TRADING
BULLETS
WITH THE
DEVIL

KIRSTEN CROSS &
MARK STEENSLAND

TRADING BULLETS WITH THE DEVIL

CEMETERY·DANCE PUBLICATIONS

Baltimore
2024

Cemetery Dance Publications
132B Industry Lane, Unit #7
Forest Hill, MD 21050
www.cemeterydance.com

Trade Paperback Edition

ISBN:
978-1-964780-12-2

Cover Artwork and Design © 2024 by Marc Green
Interior Design © 2024 by Steven Pajak

1

One sound unites mankind.
One sound is present at birth.
At death.
And at all points in between.
A heartbeat.

It's how we know we're alive. It's what binds our spirit in this world, and the next.

For a soldier staring up at the harsh Afghan sky, feeling the blood from a sniper's bullet wound seeping into her clothes, every heartbeat is cherished. Especially when she knows the medic screaming into their radio for an emergency evac isn't much older than her own beloved baby daughter. Brand new. Brand fucking new.

Beat.

The silent thudding of the helo's rotors as her ride lands in a cloud of choking dust mere meters from the hot zone, the pilot instinctively ducking as the Taliban snipers open fire.

Beat.

The ER at Bastion. Army medics efficiently working their asses off to stop her flatlining.

Beat.

The chaplain, muttering and crossing the air over her, as if to swat away the flies hovering over her soul, waiting to pounce. Gabriel Monteyo, a grunt with a grudge against the world, yelling at her to keep fighting. She still believed to this day it was his rage—not the padre's Papal patois—that kept her body and soul together. The same Gabriel Monteyo whose ass she'd saved in Al-Qa'im. Did that even the score? Was the debt repaid? Does saving someone's soul carry the same exchange rate as hauling someone's ass out of a firefight?

Beat.

Cathy. Beautiful, beautiful little Cathy. Blue eyes and curls. Smiles and kisses.

Beat.

The Lightbringers. Their incessant chanting.

Beat.

Her first glimpse of a demon. Rising slowly from a ring of fire, maw belching sulfurous gasses. A swipe of its talons opening the guts of the high priest before the stupid son of a bitch could bind it. The frantic screaming and blind panic of the brethren right up to the point she, Gabriel, and Carver filled the demon with blessed bullets and watched Baal's badass buddy explode in a shower of rotting, Hell-spawn flesh. Not something you see every day.

Beat.

That was the last time Gabriel touched a gun. The last time he embraced death as a solution. But not her. For her, it was another day at the office.

Beat.

Battle. After battle. After bloody, bloody battle.

BEAT. BEAT. BEAT.

The howling bellow of a semi's horn snapped Rebecca "Beck" Tibbot out of her heartbeat-induced trance. She hauled on the steering wheel of the jeep in time to swing the rusty piece of crap out of the way of eighteen wheels of oblivion. The semi was still blaring as it thundered past her, the wheel nuts inches from her head.

Beck didn't slow down, but she gripped the steering wheel a little bit tighter than before. She ran a hand over her face and across her blond hair, cupping the back of her neck, feeling the sweat in between her fingertips—greasy and gritty. A fine film of dust coated her aviator shades. A fine film of dread coated her soul.

In the vineyard, the monks stopped and looked, alerted by the banshee howl of the semi in full flood. They saw the jeep lurch across the lane to safety. To a man, they crossed themselves and offered a prayer of thanks for the life of the driver. The semi disappeared into the distance, but the jeep headed for the open gates. The monks, their purple-stained fingers still automatically picking the grapes from the vines, watched as the knobby tires spat a rooster-tail of dust and stones out the back of the jeep. Like a flock of doves sensing a hawk on the wing, they watched, shielding the low October sun from their eyes.

Beck powered the jeep up the gravel track towards the monastery. Her sleeveless black shirt and khaki pants a stark contrast to the monk's brown cassocks and white rope cinctures. Doves and hawks. Angels and demons.

The dark gray stones of the compound basilica felt comforting in the soft California sunshine. The glint of quartz made them shimmer, giving the whole place an ethereal feeling. The not-quite-of-this-earth sensation was quickly eradicated by the enormous backfire the Jeep let out as it slewed to a stop in the visitor parking area. The cloud of dust kicked up by the knobby tires coated the half-dozen other cars that already occupied the other spaces. The Mercedes coupe caught the worst of the detritus. Someone would need a damn good valet after this trip to Napa Valley.

Beck killed the engine and hauled the emergency brake into position to stop the ancient Jeep from rolling back and straight into a Porsche 911. Beck glanced at the ninety-thousand-dollar car as she climbed out of her five-hundred-dollar Jeep. A mischievous demon popped onto her shoulder. Should she let the brake off? Huh? Should she?

Beck shook her head and banished the demon.

She was good at that.

Banishing.

It was kind of her thing.

She patted the gun in her belt holster, made sure her shirt covered it discreetly, and walked towards the visitor center. *Packing in a monastery?* Crazy. But so was her mission. And nobody was about to get in her way.

Her boots crunched the gravel, making a noise like breakfast cereal getting walked into the carpet by a six-year-old. A blond haired, blue eyed six-year-old. All smiles and kisses.

Beat.

Cathy.

Beat.

Beautiful, innocent Cathy.

Beat.

The low-ceilinged visitor center smelled of wine, incense, and sanctimonious bullshit. Overstuffed bookshelves groaned under the weight of copies of *Great Wines of The New World* and Bibles of every kind (including a pop-up version for the kids), and pamphlets. Souvenir-laden tables with handwritten signs encouraged visitors to *Buy Me*, while rack after rack of wine rested against the coolest, north-facing wall, wax tops and elegantly printed labels hinting of the grapey goodness within.

Sitting at a small table that featured another pile of pamphlets, a cash register and a rotating rack of leather keyrings was a surprisingly young monk. He looked up from his Bible and smiled kindly at Beck. "Welcome. Welcome. Are you here for the afternoon tour?"

Beck was still taking in every little detail of the lobby. PTSD did that to a girl. Made you hypervigilant. Made you hyper-aware of every tiny little detail. That PTSD had kept her alive, so she wasn't about to ignore it now.

She stepped closer to the monk and peeled her aviators off, let her blue eyes bore into him. Watched his smile fade, then said, "No."

2

In the library, Brother Gabriel Monteyo stared at the binding of a particularly old book and smiled. He flicked a speck of dust from the fading gold-leaf title print and, tucking the book in one hand, put his other on the rail of the stepladder. This one belonged on the top shelf, where the novices wouldn't see it. A first edition copy of *Daemonologie* by King James might raise a few eyebrows in the hallowed library of a monastery in northern California. So. Out of sight, out of mind.

He heard the frantic slap of sandals on flagstones and glanced down into the wide eyes of a very startled looking Brother Marcus. Gabriel frowned. Marcus should be looking after the front desk in the visitor center.

Brother Marcus opened and closed his mouth several times and then started to apologize, gabbling his words. "Brother Gabriel, there's someone here to see you. She insists."

Gabriel shook his head and pointed at his mouth.

"Yes, yes, I know. I told her."

Gabriel waited.

The young man sighed. "She said, and God forgive me for this, she said to get your head out of your ass and get out there now."

Gabriel raised an eyebrow.

Marcus shook his head. "She says she's not leaving until you come out." He sighed again. "I believe her, Brother. I really do."

Gabriel closed his eyes and shook his head, his dark curls dancing. It was hard to tell if he was upset or laughing to himself.

"I'll have the Abbot tell her to come back."

Gabriel shook his head again and climbed down the ladder. He scooped up a yellow legal pad and a pencil from a nearby table as they headed out of the library and tried not to chuckle at the sound of Brother Marcus' size fourteens slap-slapping against the flagstones ahead of him.

3

In the visitor center, Beck sat with her ass perched on a table corner, arms crossed over her chest. She was trying to ignore the Sacramento family who were ya-ya'ing like crazy and stank of money. The teenage son, a jock with a fortune in dental correction filling his mouth, sidled over to her and gave her his best jock leer. "Hey, sugar." He smirked. "Did it hurt when you fell out of heaven?"

Beck pushed her aviators down her nose and turned a laser-beam stare that promised pain, pain, and more pain full blast at the boy. "Seriously, kid. Fuck off." She pushed the glasses back into position, crossed her arms and stared straight ahead.

"Brad." The mother yelped. "Leave the lady alone. I'm so sorry, he's at that age." She smiled nervously at Beck. "All hormones and prom queens." Mom laughed nervously.

Beck snorted. "Yeah. Ain't they all."

Mom looked confused and opened her mouth to reply when the door marked "STAFF ONLY" swung open and Brother Marcus stepped through, his best "greet the visitors" smile fixed onto his face. He headed straight for the family, welcoming them. "Sorry to have kept you waiting. Are you here for this afternoon's tour?"

"We are indeed," Brad's father said. He'd gotten a "Sarah Connor" vibe from the smoking hot blonde in the black vest and khaki pants. But right now, he wanted to get as far away from her as possible before he either mentally cheated on his wife or the shooting started.

Beck started to ask him where Gabriel was but stopped when the door opened and he came through.

She smiled, barely, and peeled her sunglasses off. "Hello, Gabriel."

He scribbled quickly on the yellow pad and held it up. "I CAN'T TALK RIGHT NOW."

"Bullshit," Beck said.

The family gasped and Brother Marcus suggested they talk outside.

"Good idea," Beck said and pushed through the door into a small garden.

The tinkling sound of running water filled the air, and the scent of honeysuckle filled her nostrils. Bees hummed in the late afternoon sun. Gabriel closed the door. They could have been the only two people in the entire world at that point. Even the sound of traffic on the nearby highway was blocked by the thick stone walls. The same quartz crystals that turned the outer basilica into a shimmering mirage as the sun's rays hit it glistened and twinkled in the garden walls too. It was magical.

Beck paused, drinking in the peace. She sighed, turned, and looked at Gabriel. He was writing again. "IT'S CALLED A SILENT RETREAT. COME BACK IN THREE DAYS WHEN IT'S OVER."

Beck shook her head. "I don't have three days."

Gabriel rolled his eyes and flipped the page over to start writing again. Beck grabbed the pad away from him.

"Cut the shit. Talk to me. I'm sure God'll forgive you."

Gabriel grabbed the pad back and wrote again. "YOU BELIEVE IN GOD NOW?"

"No. But you do. That's why I need your help. Pack a bag. I'll wait for you out front." Beck started to leave but stopped when Gabriel spoke.

"The only place I'm going is back to the library."

Beck smiled as she faced him, turning on her laser-beam stare. "You saying you forgot?"

"Forgot what?"

"The promise you made. At Al-Qa'im. Any time, you said. Anywhere. No questions. You'd be there."

Gabriel stared at Beck, a dark cast clouding his eyes. "You can't be serious?"

"Without me, you're a five-year-old pile of vulture shit in the desert."

"And without me, you'd be somewhere hotter, soldier."

"Not yet." Beck held out her hands and looked at herself.

She stared back at Gabriel. "Apart from a massive scar in the chest and a lifelong hatred of the smell of incense, still in one piece." She dropped her hands to her side. "I need you. Cathy needs you." She walked to the door, out of the little piece of heaven and back into the hell of the real world. "Outside in ten. Or I come back in here and drag you out. Soldier." She wrenched open the door and marched through it.

Gabriel watched her walk out of the lobby. He sighed again and looked up, seeking divine inspiration. Instead, he caught the gaze of the abbot, standing on the balcony. Gabriel held his arms in a "What do I do?" gesture. The abbot simply nodded and returned to the shadows of the cloister.

4

If you want to see a microcosm of all the weird shit people can be, a Walmart parking lot is the place. Even so, the sight of a monk in full cassock striding purposefully toward the doors, accompanied by a Lara Croft look-alike raised more than a few eyebrows. A group of spotty-faced youths were particularly enamored with the sight, and stared, slack jawed. One slowly raised a cellphone and there was an audible *click* as he took a picture.

Beck stopped in her tracks, turned, and stared at the kid. She muttered to Gabriel. "Wait here."

"Beck, don't. He's only a kid."

Beck ignored Gabriel and walked up to the kid, who still had his cellphone outstretched. She gently removed it from his hand, looked at the screen and swiped a couple of times. She found the photo, hit *delete*, and handed the phone to the kid. "He's kind of shy, kiddo. No photos. You know?"

The tone of her voice made clear this was not a negotiation. The Glock-shaped bulge on her waist drove home the point. "Take another photo and you're likely to get the whole wrath of God thing coming down on you. Okay?" She gave the kid a smile so bright and so chilling, all he could do was gulp and nod a couple of times in response. "Adda boy."

She spun around on her heels and headed towards Gabriel. As she reached him, she turned him to the doors and nodded. "Anyone asks, it's a Halloween costume."

"Is that what you said to that kid?"

"In a roundabout kind of way, yes."

"Really?"

"Nope. Coming?" Beck smirked as they reached the doors, which slid open with a slight hiss. The smell of middle America hit them—a blend of cheap food, cheap soap, and expensive dreams. "Men's department."

Gabriel trailed after Beck as she made her way through the crowds of shoppers. A few stared. Most didn't. Gabriel had never felt so damned self-conscious in his entire life.

5

Gabriel swooshed open the changing room curtain and stood sheepishly in front of Beck. "Well?" He held his arms out and did a three-sixty for her approval. Plaid flannel shirt, jeans, black boots. He looked every inch the average Joe.

"Perfect." Beck pushed herself off the table she'd been perching on and reached into a pocket. Flipping out a Leatherman, she opened it and selected the blade. "Hold still."

"What are you—"

"I said: hold still." She grabbed the price tag on the shirt and cut through the plastic tie. Beck did the same with the jeans, and then casually kicked the boot box back into the changing room and swished the curtain shut. "Righty, then. Let's go."

"We're not stealing this stuff. Are we?"

"Buddy, I have gas money, enough for a couple burgers and that's it. I'm guessing you're not exactly flush with cash either, right?"

Gabriel didn't know what to say.

"Good. That settles it." She grinned at Gabriel. "Makes a change from killing people, right? And everyone grabs a five-finger discount at least once in their lives from Walmart. Put this down to a life experience and come the fuck on before security makes his rounds again."

Gabriel sighed, grabbed his cassock, rolled it into a ball and trotted after Beck.

Back in the parking lot, the youths meerkatted as soon as they heard the doors open. When they saw it was the woman and the monk, they became very focused on their shoes, and very focused on avoiding catching the crazy lady's death-stare for a second time.

A woman carrying what could only be loosely described as a dog in her purse, nearly tripped over her own feet as she passed Beck. The dog yipped once, then, like the youths, thought better of it and snuggled back down into its mistress' purse. Beck had that effect on people. She could fill a room just by being there.

They finally got to the dusty old Jeep and climbed in. Gabriel tossed his cassock onto the back seat next to his pack. "You know I haven't touched a gun since our last encounter."

"I should think not." Beck pushed the key into the ignition and turned. The Jeep turned over lazily. "C'mon, c'mon, start, baby, start." The Jeep responded and coughed to life. Beck shifted into gear and released the emergency brake. "I shouldn't have thought there was much need to be armed at a monastery, was there? Unless you had an unprecedented number of violent wine thefts, that is."

Gabriel instinctively held on to the grab bar as Beck took the car lot exit at speed. He turned and looked at her. "No, you don't understand. I've made a vow."

"To God. I know."

"To never use a gun. Ever again. I'm not a killer anymore."

Beck glanced at him. "I don't need a killer. I need you and your God."

They took the on-ramp and joined the freeway. It was mid-afternoon, so the traffic was surprisingly light. Gabriel stared at the open fields and vineyards whipping past like spokes on a wheel. There was something in Beck's voice that showed a vulnerability in her otherwise iron-hard exterior. She was hurting. He looked at her. "Why?"

"Why what?"

"Why do you need me?"

"Best I don't give you any heads up on this one. So you go in with no preconceptions. Clean slate, like."

Gabriel frowned. "Okay, but at least tell me where we're going, huh?"

Wordlessly, Beck pointed at the black skyline of the city. It reminded Gabriel of a line of giant tombstones. The city was where souls went to die. There were things there, dark things, which shunned the daylight and the clinical monotony of city life. Things that lived in the sewers and the broken-toothed, decayed factories down by the docks. There were places even the rats didn't go in that godforsaken place.

After another half hour, Beck took the exit ramp off the freeway and headed through the city center. The skyscrapers formed canyons of glass and steel, reflecting an image of their passing. Gabriel felt like every window was an eye, watching them, judging them, and finding them unworthy. Despite the wide boulevards and spacious squares, it felt claustrophobic and suffocating. Why was he here? Okay. Let's go fish.

"So."

Beck didn't take her eyes off the road.

"You ask the others? What about Velasquez? Or Carver?"

Beck glanced at him. Even behind the aviators, he could see her expression.

"And they said yes?"

"They owed me. Same as you."

Gabriel frowned again. "Sounds to me like you're calling in a ton of favors."

"Every last marker."

Gabriel felt a knot tighten in his guts. This was bad. Real bad. "So where are they?"

Beck slewed around a corner into a warehouse yard. The Jeep skidded to a halt by an unassuming burgundy door. The tires spat dust and debris into the air and Gabriel slammed a hand into the dash to avoid going through the windscreen. Beck hauled on the emergency brake and turned the engine off. She twisted in her seat and pointed at the burgundy door.

"In there."

Gabriel stared at the door, the dried-blood-colored paint and the grease stains, the tarnished push handle and the surprisingly new-looking security camera sitting over the top.

The knot in his stomach ratcheted up a notch.

An old homeless man wandered past and nodded at Beck. "Hey Dave. How's tricks?"

Dave pointed at his shopping cart full of plastic bags. "Got myself one heap of cans to trade in, miss Beck." Dave grinned a black-toothed smile. "Should get me a meal and a little something to keep out the chill, you know?"

Beck gave the old guy a soft smile and reached into a pocket. She pulled out a folded twenty and held it up. "Seen anyone around?"

"Just your friends, miss Beck. Nobody else. I keeps looking for you. Like you asked."

"I know, Dave. I know. And I'm grateful." She held out the twenty and Dave cautiously looked at it before holding up a grubby hand and gently taking it from her.

"You're a good lady, miss Beck."

"And you're a good man, Davy. Take yourself off and get something to eat." Beck hopped out of the Jeep and gave Dave a thumbs up. "See you around, soldier."

Davy waved as he wandered away, chuckling to himself, pushing a cart that contained his entire world.

Gabriel climbed out the other side. "That was our gas money, wasn't it?"

"He needs it more than I do." Beck grabbed Gabriel's pack from the back seat and tossed it to him. He caught it, stuffed his cassock into it, and slung the bag over his shoulder. Gabriel looked at the only other vehicles in the yard: a black Range Rover with tinted windows, fat tires, and a menacing road presence designed to scare the bejesus out of the average coupe. Next to it was a cheerful little yellow Mini that Gabriel instinctively knew had a trunk stuffed full of danger.

"Let me guess." He pointed to the Range Rover. "Carver." His finger moved towards the Mini. "And Velasquez."

Beck shook her head. "Nope."

Gabriel's eyes widened. "What? No way Carver fits in that tiny little thing."

"Who knows with that guy? He's defied a lot of laws in his time. Don't see why physics should be any different. Besides, I'd guess he sits on the back seat to drive. You coming?" Beck wandered over to the burgundy door and pulled it open.

Gabriel sighed, shook his head, and followed her.

6

The interior of the building was not what Gabriel expected. It looked more like a frat house, with band posters on the walls, cheap patio chairs that looked like they'd seen the bottom of at least two swimming pools, a vintage Pacman tabletop machine that would send any hipster's heart a-fluttering, and a sagging couch even Toothless Dave would probably pass on. An old console TV sat in the corner. It looked broken.

"What is this?" Gabriel noticed a strong smell of weed and a distinctively sticky sensation underfoot.

"Band practice space. Cheap. Out of the way. And soundproof."

The soundproof bit disturbed Gabriel. But before he could mention it, a shout grabbed his attention. "Gabriel Monteyo, you god-fearing son of a bitch." The expletive was followed by a deep laugh. A huge pair of arms wrapped around Gabriel's shoulders, and he could feel his feet leaving the sticky floor.

"Carver, I can't breathe. Ease up. Ease up."

Carver, all six foot four and 240 pounds of solid muscle, laughed again and pulled back. He slapped Gabriel on the shoulder. "My man. Where's the cassock?"

"In the duffle. The civvies were Beck's idea." Gabriel gave Carver a huge grin. "You're looking sharp as ever, big guy."

Carver, dressed in expensive black slacks, a white dress shirt and black jacket, did a sweep down of himself. "Gotta keep up appearances, am I right?"

Gabriel laughed. "Not really my thing. Where are the dreads?"

Carver ran a hand over his short black hair, his face momentarily serious. "Fire hazard, dude. Fire hazard."

"I told you Beck wouldn't let him wear the robe. You owe me twenty." The voice was soft and feminine. "Hey, priest." Velasquez peered around the bulk of Carver. "You look well."

Carver stepped aside and let Gabriel embrace the woman. He almost swamped her five foot two, slender frame, boosted to five four thanks to the two-inch heels on her brown boots. Gabriel could feel the outline of a Glock 9mm tucked into her jeans as he hugged her. The little firecracker always carried.

As she hugged him back, she held a hand towards Carver

and snapped her fingers. Carver sighed, reached into his jacket pocket, and pulled out a wad of notes. He peeled off a twenty and handed the folded bill to her. She smiled, stepped back from Gabriel's embrace, and went to tuck the bill in her bra. It got a few inches from her neck and was whipped out of her hand by Beck.

"Sorry, kiddo. Had to give Toothless Dave a twenty. You know how it is."

"Damn it."

Carver grinned. "So you have the whole cassock thing, then? You wanna give me a catwalk later so I can get a selfie with a real live monk?"

"You're weird."

"We're all weird, brother." Carver laughed again. "Man, it's good to see you. Even if it did cost me twenty bucks."

"You'll get your reward in heaven." Gabriel looked back at Velasquez, who gave him a fleeting smile.

"Mi hermano."

Gabriel returned the smile. "Mi hermana." He hugged her again.

"Easy there. You're a man of the cloth now." Carver let out a guffaw. "You're leading him astray, you harlot."

Gabriel smiled sheepishly. "So. We getting the band back together or what?"

Suddenly, all the jollity, the happy reunion, the old friends together again—it all evaporated like dawn mist. Carver's usually smiling face was dark. "She didn't tell you."

Gabriel shook his head. "You know Beck. Orders first, questions never. Like always. I'm surprised you guys didn't have a little wager on that too."

Before either of them could respond, Beck's quiet voice cut

through like a knife. "You got the whole bell, book and candle package with you?"

"Bible and crucifix."

"Get them and follow me." Beck opened a door and walked into another room.

Gabriel looked at Velasquez. "You got a vampire back there or something?"

Without a hint of a smile, Velasquez answered. "Or something."

Gabriel, trying to ignore the knot in his stomach that had returned and was currently trying to turn his intestines into a string of sausages, opened his pack and grabbed his battered old Bible and crucifix. Carver and Velasquez dropped the banter and followed him through the door, Velasquez's hand instinctively hovering over her Glock. She was ready.

Carver was also carrying a 9mm. He was itching for action and also ready.

Was Gabriel, though? Would that tattered old Bible and woodworm-infested crucifix be enough for what he was about to face?

7

The plinking noise of fluorescent lights flickering into life revealed a drab, windowless room. The walls were soundproofed with layers of heavy, dull green carpet. This wasn't the kind of studio you'd find a major band rehearsing in. This was a studio where punk bands who'd scraped up enough money for one session (minus the sound engineer) thrashed out five shitty, tinny little tunes for a mini-album with piss-poor graphics and even worse sound quality. Mic stands were lined up on one side next to a stack of beaten-up amplifiers and a snake pit of loosely coiled black cables.

Gabriel stopped at the doorway. Two things hit him. The first was the pungent smell of stale beer, underpinned with the sweet stink of herbal cigarettes from an overflowing ashtray perched on top of one of the amps. And the second was that there was a man duct-taped to a makeshift crucifix in the middle of the room.

The man, who couldn't have been a day over forty-five, was dressed in smart-casual clothes. White jeans paired up with a dark blue polo top, accessorized with Italian shoes and an expensive watch. If not for the fact he was blindfolded, gagged, and crucified, he could've walked straight out of the local country club.

Gabriel stared for a few seconds at the man and then turned to Beck. "What the hell?"

Beck's face was grim. "Gabe, meet Kip Marton."

"Well, thanks for the introduction, I feel a whole lot better now." Gabe slammed the Bible down on a rickety old three-legged table that barely held its own against the onslaught of the angry monk. "I'll say again, what the actual fuck?"

"Calm down."

"Calm down?" Gabriel's voice went up a notch. "You have a man taped to a crucifix in the middle of a soundproofed room and you're telling me to calm down? This is kidnapping. A major felony."

"It's not a kidnapping. It's an interrogation."

"Oh, well that makes all the damn difference then." Gabriel sighed. "We're not in the ME anymore. Kip here ain't Isis. I doubt if he even cheats on his taxes, I mean, look at him."

Gabriel turned to Beck and laid a hand on her shoulder. "Babes, this is wrong. I know it's wrong. You know it's wrong. Even if the guy was a terrorist, this is still wrong." He took his hand away and swore. "Fuck. Fuck. You hear that? Five years and not one expletive passed my lips. Three hours with you and it's like I never quit, for Christ's sake."

He turned to Velasquez and Carver. "And I can't even begin to believe you guys are okay with all this."

Velasquez answered softly. "There's good reason."

"What? What good reason?" He waved an arm at the limp figure. "What good reason could possibly justify this?"

"They have Cathy." Beck's voice was flat.

Gabriel reeled. He felt like he'd been slapped. "What? Are you serious?"

"Yes." Again, that monotone, flat, emotionless answer.

Gabe paced and then spun on his heels. "So what's Chad—"

"Kip."

"Kip. Okay, what's Kip here got to do with it?"

"He's a Lightbringer." Beck's voice didn't give anything away.

"That's not helping me understand what's going on here."

Beck stalked to the tethered Kip and stared at him. "He's a member of some strip-mall church my scumbag of an ex-husband joined last year. He moved in with them after the divorce. Took Cathy too."

"A church." Gabriel's voice wavered.

"Yeah."

"A strip-mall church."

Beck turned her laser-beam stare up a notch and it bored into Gabriel cranked up to eleven. "A strip-mall church that's into some seriously weird shit." She focused onto Kip. "Ain't that right?"

Gabriel crossed his arms. "Define weird shit."

"Well, how about stockpiling guns? Bigging up the whole 'Doomsday is upon us' and 'He rises from beneath' bullshit?"

"So the old Waco vibe, then?"

Beck nodded, her focus on Kip. "Yeah. Only cranked up a gear or ten."

Gabriel picked up his Bible from the three-legged table and held it tight. "Then you don't need me. You need the feds."

Carver laid a hand on Gabriel's shoulder. "It's more complicated than that."

Gabriel faced his friend. "I appreciate they've got Cathy, I really do. But are you sure she's in danger? I mean, she's with her pop, right? And if they are holding her against her will then it's a federal case, brother. Not an ecumenical one. Or at least Family Services." He smiled benignly at his friends. "Sorry, guys, but I'm out. If you won't call the cops, I will." He walked over to Beck and squeezed her shoulder. "I'm gonna get an Uber, okay? Drop by the monastery sometime and let me know how it went."

He turned and started to walk out of the room. As he passed Carver and Velasquez he smiled. "Good to see you guys again. God bless."

As he reached the door, a low, throaty chuckle stopped him in is tracks. Rising and falling, it sounded as if someone were reading the Sunday newspaper funnies and laughing happily at the escapades of Charlie Brown and Snoopy. For some reason, it made Gabriel's skin crawl. He spun around, an angry glare on his face. He focused his ire on the huge figure of his friend. "Something funny about this, Carver?"

Carver, his face stony, shook his head. He jerked a thumb towards Kip.

The crucified man had managed to wriggle his gag out of his mouth and the rag now hung limply around his neck. Perfect teeth and full lips were split into a wide grin. The chuckles grew louder.

"Here we go again." Velasquez and Carver backed up, Glocks already in their hands.

"What?" Gabriel felt a tight knot twisting in his stomach again. Only this time the son of a bitch had barbed wire mixed in with it, to add interest.

"Why do you think we've got him tied up like that?" Carver sounded unsure, concerned.

Gabriel had never heard his friend sound so worried. The knot in his gut tightened a notch. He noticed Beck had also backed well away from the increasingly maniacal laughter and was heading towards the door. Gabriel assumed she was making a run for it.

He was wrong.

Beck quietly closed the door as Kip's laughing reached a tipping point and flipped over into a screeching howl that sounded like a lynx getting ready for the fight of its life. The feline screech almost had substance, scraping down Gabriel's skin like claws.

The fluorescent light started flickering. Kip stopped screeching and the entire makeshift crucifix started to vibrate, setting up a clattering hum against the floor.

"You're up, Gabe." Beck's voice came from behind the monk.

"What?"

The lights went out, plunging the room into thick darkness.

"Now would be a good time." There was a sense of urgency in Beck's voice.

Gabriel, still trying to get his bearings in the blackness and attempting to ignore the increasingly loud clattering of the crucifix as it vibrated, clutched his Bible like a comfort blanket. "For what, exactly?"

"Are you shitting me?" Carver's voice cut through the noise and blackness. "Exorcise the fuck out of him."

Gabriel rallied. This, he could do. "I need light."

The blaze from a cellphone illuminated Gabriel, like a spotlight.

It also illuminated Kip, somehow mere inches from Gabriel's face.

Jet black eyes bored into the monk's own, filled with pure evil. He opened his mouth and roared. Behind him, the crucifix continued vibrating, the restraints now in tatters.

"JESUS." Gabriel stumbled back, knocking the phone out of Beck's hand and tripping over that damned three-legged table. His Bible flew out of his hand and landed on the floor. The pages, illuminated by the still-shining cellphone, fluttered and turned in an unseen breeze. They came to rest at Revelation 13:18. The words blazed into Gabriel's soul "Here is wisdom. Let him that hath understanding count the number of the beast: for it is the number of a man; and his number is six hundred threescore and six."

Carver shoved Gabriel to one side as he barreled past. The huge man wrapped his arms around Kip and lifted him clear of the floor, dragging him backwards. Kip, held like a ragdoll in Carver's muscular arms, simply laughed again. His eyes changed from black pits to glowing, fire-filled orbs. He tipped his head back and began to chant in Latin—deep, guttural tones filled with menace.

"Now, Gabe, NOW, for fuck's sake, NOW." Beck grabbed the Bible and slammed it into Gabriel's chest.

"I don't know how long I can hold him." Carver's voice was tension-taut, and he flexed his massive arms tighter around Kip's chest, struggling to pin the slim man's arms to his sides.

"I can't find the passage."

"Then fucking improvise." The note of desperation in Carver's voice was clear.

Gabriel looked at Kip, snarled, and leapt forward. He grabbed the man's hair and pulled his face level with his own. Gabriel made the sign of the cross on Kip's forehead, between those glowing eyes and shouted. "In the name of the Father, and of the Son, and of the Holy Ghost, I bind you, unclean spirit, and banish you back into the outer darkness." Gabriel swung the Bible in a backhand arc and slammed it into Kip's face.

Kip roared and burst free of Carver's grip, sending the big man and Gabriel flying back in opposite directions. A sound of all the tormented souls of Hell screaming with one voice filled the room. Beck, Carver, Gabriel, and Velasquez all dropped to their knees, trying to cover their ears from the howl of Hell. Blood dripped from Beck's nose, and she screwed her eyes tight shut, trying to block out the noise.

Then...

Silence.

The fluorescent light plinked and pinged a couple of times, flickered, and came on, crackling quietly.

Kip was secured on the wooden crucifix as if nothing had happened. His head drooped, his chin resting on his chest. He looked drained, corpse-like. It was only the shallow raising and falling of his chest that signified the man was still alive.

Gabriel rubbed his head as he staggered to his feet and held a hand to Beck. She grabbed it and he hauled her up. "Okay. What just happened here?" He jerked his head towards the still-flaccid form of Kip Marton.

Beck brushed herself down. "Number two on the list of weird shit." Ignoring the corpse-like Marton, Beck beckoned to the team, and they wandered into the front room.

Beck walked to a pile of amps in the corner and picked up a leaflet. She turned and held it to Gabriel.

Gabriel took the leaflet. On the front was a picture of a typical European Jesus. The only bits that weren't standard Sunday school graphics were the orange laser beams shooting out of his eyes that morphed into flaming letters proclaiming, "THE FIRE IS COMING."

Gabriel looked at Beck. "I don't remember this from the Sermon on the Mount." He turned the leaflet over and back again. "And that is definitely not the Jesus I know and love."

"Pity. We could've done with him in Al-Qa'im." Beck shrugged.

Gabriel glared at Beck. "Look, I know Christ is a joke to you, but it's a big part of my life now. So I'd appreciate reigning in the blasphemy, okay?"

Beck looked genuinely remorseful for a second. "Sorry. I didn't mean that."

"Apology accepted." Gabriel turned the leaflet over. "Light-bringer. That was the name given to Lucifer."

"So they're devil worshipers?" Velasquez shrugged. "We kinda got that when Chad here started doing the whole *Exorcist* thing."

"It's more complicated than that, to be honest." Gabriel started reading the pamphlet.

"That was a demon you bitch-slapped with a Bible, though, right?" Carver rotated his shoulder and winced.

"Well if it wasn't then that guy has one hell of a food allergy." Gabriel looked at Beck. "Babes, I still say you should go to the feds."

"And tell them what?" Beck took the pamphlet back. "My asshole ex has full custody of Cathy. He can take her wherever he wants to, as long as it's not out of state."

Gabriel frowned. "I thought the courts favored the mom."

Velasquez shook her head. "Not when the mom has a very public meltdown, punches a cop into next week, and it goes viral on YouTube."

Gabriel looked at Beck, who simply shrugged. "I was having a bad day."

"Really?"

"I told you it was complicated."

Gabriel sighed and ran his hand through his curly hair. "If you explain Cathy's in danger, they'll have to listen."

Beck rounded on Gabriel, her blue eyes flashing in anger. "And say what, exactly?" She pointed at Kip. "Would you believe that shit if you hadn't seen it with your own eyes?"

Carver muttered quietly. "Hell, dude, even I don't believe it and I was holding the son of a bitch when you hit him."

Velasquez spoke quietly. "Plus, telling the feds that she's scared her daughter, who as far as they're concerned, she abandoned, is at risk from a church that feeds homeless people and holds yard sales to raise money for immigrant families sounds even crazier than 'hey, you know demons are real, right?' shit." She shrugged. "Face it: we're on our own on this one."

"We're on a time limit, too." Beck wandered over to a small hotel fridge and opened it. She pulled out four bottles of water and tossed three of them to the team. "Kip told me 'nothing would matter after dawn on Thursday'. That gives us less than thirty-six hours." She unscrewed the top of the water bottle and took a long swig.

Gabriel took a drink of his own water bottle and frowned. "What happens then?"

"That's when the fire is coming." Carver cracked open his bottle and downed the contents in one go.

"Fire?"

Carver shrugged and wiped the back of his hand across his mouth. "You got me."

Gabriel frowned. "Okay. So does Kip know where Cathy is?"

"No, but he's all we've got right now." Beck's voice had that edge of desperation again.

Gabriel took another swig from his water and looked at Beck. "We better find out what he does know then, huh?"

"So you're in?" Beck looked hopeful for the first time that day.

Gabriel smiled at her. "Of course I am. Anytime, anywhere. No questions. That's what we agreed six years ago, right?" He put a gentle arm around her shoulders. "Now let's go see if Kip can help us find Cathy."

8

"I don't remember any of this."

Kip Marton sat shaking on a chair. After Gabriel's protestations and assurances that the guy was demon-free, Carver had thrown half a bottle of water in the guy's face to wake him up, examined his eyes carefully for any sign of possession by prizing his eyelids wide open, and finally satisfied, cut the guy loose.

Now Kip, nursing a Bible-induced black eye and wiping

dried blood from his nostrils with a damp tissue, sat in a chair, painfully aware he was the center of attention for four very dangerous-looking mercs.

"Nothing?" Beck pushed.

"Nothing. I mean, you say I used to live at the place I was showing you?"

Beck responded. "The whole church did. Until a week ago, that is."

"What happened then?" Kip briefly looked at Gabriel. "You don't have any aspirin, do you? I have one hell of a headache. Did somebody hit me with something heavy?"

Gabriel looked sheepish and reached into a pocket. He pulled out a jar of aspirin and tossed the bottle to Kip, who gave Gabriel a nervous "thank-you" smile.

Beck carried on talking while Kip swallowed the pills. "The place is up for sale now. I got you to meet me there by pretending I wanted to buy the property on behalf of another church. Anything coming back to you, kiddo?"

"No, and could you not call me kiddo? I'm older than you are, lady." Kip frowned and rubbed the swollen side of his face.

Beck's eyes flashed. "Maybe another bruise might help you remember, kiddo?" She grabbed Kip's polo shirt and telescoped her arm, ready for a punch.

Gabriel captured her arm and shook his head. "That's not gonna help."

"It'll make me feel a whole lot better about things." Beck struggled with Gabriel, who nodded to Carver.

"A little help here?"

Carver pushed himself off the sagging couch and bear hugged Beck. "Gabe's right. You catch more flies with honey rather than vinegar."

"The fuck does that even mean?" Beck struggled briefly, sighed, and reluctantly allowed herself to be escorted to the couch.

Carver pointed at the seat. "Sit. You've had your turn. Let Gabriel have a shot."

"How can he not remember me putting a bag over his head?" Beck muttered.

"Dunno. I know I would, though. Am I right, sista?" The two women bumped fists.

Kip looked at Gabriel. "You're not gonna punch me, are you?"

Gabriel ignored the chuckle from Carver and shook his head. "No, Kip. We need information. A little girl's life could depend on it."

Kip looked worried. "Really? Look, man, if there's a kid in trouble, I'll do everything I can to help you. For sure. But I swear, I'm telling you everything I know." He threw a glare at Beck. "Right up to the point you say you put a bag over my head, you freak."

"Okay. That's it. Can I hit him now? Please?" Beck stood up and toppled back into the seat as Velasquez grabbed her arm and pulled her down.

Gabriel ignored Beck and focused on Kip. "Okay, let's take a break. You want some more water?" Kip nodded. "Velasquez, would you mind?"

"On it." Velasquez hopped up and crossed over to the mini fridge. "Yeah, we're out. There's a store a block away. I'll be five minutes." She stared at Beck. "Got that twenty?"

Beck sagged.

"Hand it over, girlfriend." Velasquez grinned as Beck slapped the note into her hand. "Anyone want eats?"

"Just water."

Velasquez grinned again. "Okie dokie. Back in a bit." She vanished through the outer door, letting it slam shut behind her.

Gabriel looked at Beck. "Can we talk?" He nodded to the door. Beck stood up and stalked out, throwing one last 'I'll be back' look at Kip. "Carver, can you keep an eye on our guest?"

"No problem."

Gabriel led Beck out of the room and into the short corridor between the front room and the main door. He kept his voice low. "I believe him."

Beck snorted. "Yeah. Because you want me to let him go."

"No, because I know more about this whole ethereal shooting match than you do. It's quite common for the host to have no recollection whatsoever of a demonic possession."

"What, right up to the point where the priest clobbers them with a Bible? Or because he's acting all preppy-innocent-Kip right now and asking you for aspirin?" Beck crossed her arms. "Because Damien in there didn't act possessed when I met him at the property, either."

"I get that. But it's like suicide bombers. You don't know who they are right up to the moment they show you the belt and the detonator."

"So what you're saying is Kip wasn't in control of himself?"

"Nope. The thing inside him was pulling the strings. Until we flushed him out."

"With the whole clobbering, right?" Beck flashed a grin.

"Sheesh, you are not gonna let that one go, are you?" Gabriel sighed. "Exactly. Now Kip feels like he's woken up from a particularly bad cheese dream, he has a black eye he can't explain, and some crazy lady keeps threatening him. You see why he's feeling a little uncooperative right now?"

Beck visibly drooped. "Then he can't tell me where Cathy is."

Gabriel shook his head. "I get the feeling if he could, he would. But hey, this whole exorcism thing isn't exactly a precise science. Let's keep pushing and see, okay?"

Beck nodded. "Okay."

The exterior door opened, and Velasquez stood in the frame, holding a six-pack of water, and chewing on a Twizzler. "Hey Beck? There's some guy out front. He's with a cop."

"Shit." Beck glanced at Gabriel, reached behind, and pulled her sidearm out. She slid the bolt back to check the chamber.

"Beck."

"Don't worry. I won't shoot him. Unless I really have to, okay?" Beck tucked the gun back in her waistband, draped her t-shirt over it and fixed a smile on her face.

9

The cop looked bored. The man with him looked anxious, despite his attempt to model himself on a Hollywood interpretation of a Colombian drug lord complete with Fedora, dark glasses, and huge medallion tangled in his remarkably dense chest hair. The cop, all fresh-faced Dudley Do-Right with a badge, scratched behind his ear and glanced at his watch.

Beck kept the smile fixed in place and walked towards them,

swinging her hips a bit more than she would normally. The ruse worked—to an extent. The wannabe drug lord tipped his sunglasses down and peered over the top of them in appreciation. The cop still looked bored. He'd seen a thousand women pull that one. Besides, his boyfriend back home had a way better set of hips than this chick.

"Hey, mister Perry." Beck's voice was girly and light. "What's up?"

Mister Perry pushed the glasses back into place and tried the whole mean-and-moody angry landlord routine. "Save it. I got cameras all over in here. You think I wouldn't see what you've been doing?"

"I have no idea what you're talking ab—"

"Sweet-cheeks, you ain't just playing rock and roll in there, are you? I called the cops. You're busted, bitch. Is he still in the practice room?"

The "sweet-cheeks" quip was logged for future reference, as was the "bitch" comment. Beck struggled to keep the fixed smile in place. "Who?"

The cop, now convinced he was about to call through a 10-22 disregard rather than a full-blown hostage situation, stepped forward. "Ma'am, this gentleman seems to think you have a man tied up and being held against his will in there. I'll ask you straight. Is that the case? Do I need to call the FBI here?"

"Oh, don't be ridiculous." Beck gave a tinkling little laugh. "Do I look like the kind of girl who'd do something like that?"

The cop looked at her. "Honestly? Yes." He held his thumb and forefinger slightly apart. "Little bit."

"Everything okay?" Carver loomed through the doorway, followed by Gabriel, Velasquez, still sucking on her Twizzler, and a casual-looking Kip.

"Fine. A misunderstanding, isn't that right, Mister Perry?" Beck turned her fixed smile onto the landlord, who shifted uncomfortably.

Kip stepped forward. "Officer, I apologize. We were setting up a shoot for the album cover. I'm supposed to be a middle-class junkie doing the whole restrained intervention vibe. Admittedly, it's a little on the dark side, but as you can see—" He held his arms out and gave the cop a bright smile. "—no needle marks, no problem. All okay here."

The cop sighed and turned to Perry. "Is that the man, sir?"

"Well, yes, but—"

"Then I think we're done here, don't you?" The cop spoke to Kip. "Sir, I suggest if you're gonna go for the whole dark and moody dystopian cover shoot, then maybe try giving the landlord here a heads-up first? That kinda thing can freak people out a bit, you know?"

"Absolutely, officer, and thank you. Will do." Kip smiled brightly again.

"Okay then. Good luck with the album. What's the band called?"

Beck responded, her grin still rigidly fixed to her face. It was starting to hurt. "The Lightbringers."

The cop thought about that for a moment. "Cool name."

"We thought so too." The grin flickered with the sheer effort of being held in place for far, far too long.

The cop turned to the landlord. "Everything seems to be okay, sir. You get any more problems, maybe you'll want to check them out yourself first rather than dialing nine-one-one straight away? You know what these musicians can be like."

Perry looked bemused. "Is that it? I mean, seriously?"

"Sir, there's nothing more I can do here. No crime has been committed."

Perry spluttered. "But... but... they can't stay here."

"You don't need me to kick them out." The cop opened his car door. "You folks take care now." He climbed into the black and white and slammed the driver door shut. The car spluttered into life, kicking up a cloud of dust as it turned out of the yard and off down the street.

"You donut-eating asshole." Perry hurled abuse at the car as it sped away. He refocused on the group, trying his best to look as intimidating as possible. "Do I need to say it?"

Gabriel shook his head. "No, sir. Thanks for the use of your studio. We'll go now."

"Yeah, and you ain't getting no refund, neither." Perry dragged out a bunch of keys. "Get your stuff and git."

Beck realized that the smile she'd been desperately maintaining for the past ten minutes could now be filed under "pending" and her face took on its resting "fuck around and find out" demeanor. "Grab your gear, guys. We're outta here." She turned to Kip, carefully making sure Perry couldn't see her face. "You coming with?"

Kip, playing his part perfectly, nodded. "Absolutely. I've got some great ideas for the inside cover."

Beck mouthed "Don't push it" at him. "Okay, then," she said in clear earshot of Perry. "I know a great location near an old strip mall downtown we can check out." Her stare hardened. "I think it used to be an old church."

10

Beck watched the team head back into the studio to grab their gear. Gabriel studied her, smiling gently.

"What?"

"That's the most restrained I've seen you in a long time." Gabriel chuckled.

"Was it your idea to rope Kip in on the whole photoshoot ruse?"

"Of course. I've always been the brains in this operation."

Beck let a smile flicker across her face. Brief, but there. "That's the second time you've saved my ass today."

"Who's keeping count?"

"I am." The smile vanished as quickly as it came, and Beck stared at her feet. "I need you, Gabe. More than Carver, more than Velasquez. I need you." She kicked a stone, sending it bouncing across the yard, leaving a trail of dust in its wake. Beck looked up and locked her gaze with Gabriel's. "My daughter's like your cassock. She's the only thing that's real to me anymore. She's the only thing that gets me past the sick shit we did. The only thing that makes it right. Please. Don't let them take that away from me."

Gabriel wrapped his arms around her. "Shush." He kissed her forehead gently. "You don't need to explain it to me." He hugged her again. "I admit, I was ready to go home. I tried to leave all this behind a long time ago. Funny, it has a way of biting you on the ass when you least expect it to, doesn't it?"

Beck started to stammer an apology, but Gabriel shushed her again. "That's not a reprimand. It's a fact. And now that we know what we're up against, we can beat it. We can get Cathy back. Together. Okay?"

Beck looked into his kind brown eyes, searching for a shred of hope. For a split second, she found it. Her heart pounded in her chest and the images crashed in like a stampede.

Cathy, all kisses, and curls.

The helo, hovering overhead as she bled out in the Afghan desert.

The semi, thundering towards her outside the monastery.

Gabe, slamming his tattered Bible into the face of a roaring demon.

Bullets.

Blood.

So much blood...

Her legs buckled and Gabriel caught her. She felt his strong arms holding her up. From a distance, his voice cut through the dark fog that had wrapped itself around her brain. "When did you last eat?"

The strength returned to her legs, and she pushed herself up. The here and now came back into sharp focus. She pushed Gabriel away. "I'm okay." She turned and paced. "I'll cut Kip loose now."

Gabriel shook his head. "No. He's still the best lead we've got. Besides, the guy's got a good heart. He wants to help. And I think we owe him a little closure, don't you?"

Beck carried on pacing. "How's he gonna help if he can't remember anything? He's dead weight."

"Give him time." Gabriel ran a hand through his curls. "Look, it's been a pretty intense few hours. We need to regroup. My folks' place isn't far. We could all do with a home-cooked meal about now, you think?"

Beck relented. Too many emotions were fighting inside her. She needed someone else to make decisions until she got back under control. Gabriel was her wingman. Always had been, always would be. She stopped mid-pace and nodded. The others walked out of the studio. "Carver. Velasquez. You guys follow me. Kip, you ride with me and Gabe."

Carver opened the trunk of the Mini and threw in an armful of weapons. He slammed the trunk shut. "Where to, boss?"

"Rancho Monteyo."

Carver nodded. "Copy that."

"You want I should throw a grenade in there?" Velasquez jerked her head towards the studio. "Place is full of bad juju."

Beck shook her head. "No and what is wrong with you?"

Velasquez grinned. "Just thought a bit of purification would be a good idea, is all. My bad." She wrenched open the door of the black Range Rover and hopped in, slamming the door shut behind her. The tinted window slid down, and Velasquez's grinning face appeared, a new Twizzler dangling from the corner of her mouth like a cherry-colored cigar. "Wagons roll."

Gabriel watched as Carver folded himself carefully into the Mini. "Man alive, if I hadn't seen it with my own eyes, I wouldn't have thought it possible."

"Told you," Beck said as she swung into the driver's seat of the Jeep, letting Kip scramble into the back. The Jeep sputtered to life and the transmission protested loudly as Beck shifted. "Let's go."

Gabriel stood for a second, a flood of memories swirling around him. He'd been here so many times before. He'd sworn Baal was the last time. Yet, here they were, all over again.

Anytime.

Anywhere.

No questions.

He sighed and vaulted into the passenger seat of the Jeep. Beck gassed it. Carver and Velasquez followed.

In the shadows, Toothless Dave watched their convoy go. A smile spread over his lips, and he waved his hand up and down, then side to side. For a split second, a blazing white cross hung in the air before evaporating like morning mist. Toothless Dave slowly lowered his hand and the smile vanished. "Good hunting, Beck."

11

As the sun set over the hot and gritty city, the three vehicles sped along the highway. Traffic was light, and they were making good progress, finally leaving the suffocating claustrophobia of the urban sprawl behind them. The highway climbed upwards towards the mountains and the air temperature dropped. Acres of cornfields, vineyards, and orchards flashed past in a pastoral blur. Beck and Gabriel sat up front, staring at the white lines that punctuated the black tarmac, flashing underneath the Jeep like an asphalt heartbeat.

In the back of the Jeep, Kip stared at the landscape. The green glow from the instrument panel gave his skin a sickly pallor. Inside, his tainted soul felt heavy as he struggled to remember the details of what had happened to him over the last twenty-four hours.

"Did you hear what I said?" Beck's sharp voice cut through his solitary musings.

"I'm sorry, what?"

"She was talking to you," Gabriel said. "Asking if anything was coming back yet."

Kip pinched the bridge of his nose. "Little bits. They're kinda disjointed at the moment, but there are things. They're hazy, but look, I'm having a real hard time trying to wrap my head around all this."

"I'm sure you are, but Cathy's about to have a much, much harder time if you don't start coming through with some intel." Beck glanced in the driver's mirror back at Kip. "You look like hell."

"Is that supposed to be funny?"

Gabriel pivoted in his seat. "Nobody's blaming you." He threw a pointed look at Beck, who kept on driving and let Gabriel conduct this part of the interrogation. Good cop, bad cop. It was a cliché but man, did it work when the good cop was a monk.

Gabriel focused his attention on Kip. "You've been through a tough one. We get you're messed up with this, we really do. It's a hell of a surprise when you commit to something and it turns out not what you expected it to be, right?"

Kip nodded. "Yeah. But I shoulda known."

"Why?" Gabriel took his time. Press gently. Let the guy open up at his own speed.

"Because my brother warned me. He'd read bad things about the church on the 'net. I was so deep in, I told him it was the godless media tearing us down. We were the good guys. Doing more than singing Hallelujah on a Sunday morning We fed the homeless. Sponsored immigrant families."

"Okay. So when did it all change?"

"After Pastor Reid saw the angel."

"Angel?"

"I know, it sounds crazy."

Gabriel smiled. "You're talking to a monk. We're all about the angels. I'm even named after one."

"You're not like any monk I've ever met."

"And how many of us have you met?"

Kip frowned. "You're the first, I guess."

Gabriel smiled. "Then how do you know we're not all groovy, totally cool guys with blistering one-liners and sporting snappy Walmart workwear when we're off duty?"

"Are you ever off duty?"

Gabriel's smiled faded. "No. It's kind of a twenty-four-seven, on-call job. Now, tell me about this angel your Pastor saw."

Kip's frown deepened. "He said it was standing on the mountain like a tongue of fire. His words, man, not mine. He said his name was Malphas, and that he'd burn up everyone but those who know where the fire will not go." As he spoke the words, Kip's eyes took on a glazed, unfocused look that disturbed Gabriel.

"And that's due to happen on Thursday, right? That's what you said. Dawn on Thursday." Beck's matter-of-fact tone cut through the moment.

Kip's eyes refocused and he swallowed. "Did I? That must be why they moved camp, then. The Pastor said he was waiting for Malphas to show him the way."

"The way?"

"To the mountain." Kip cupped his face in his hands. "I was only a minion, one of the congregation. I didn't see Malphas. I didn't know about it until the Pastor started a full-scale fire and damnation sermon. It was so intense, so overwhelming. I felt like I couldn't breathe. I went outside to get some air, and the next thing I know, I'm with you people." He looked pointedly at Beck. "You kidnapped the wrong guy, lady."

Beck glanced at Gabriel, who nodded. "I'm sorry. I really am."

Kip sat back. "I know you are. I can hear it in your voice. Look, I'm not a bad person. I have family. Nephews and nieces. If one of them was in trouble, I'd help any way I could. So I'll do everything I can for you."

Beck's grip tightened on the steering wheel. "Okay. Thanks."

"Sure," Kip said and turned his attention to the landscape. Gabriel pivoted in his seat and stared ahead. He knew when to stop pushing. They wouldn't get anything more out of Kip for the moment.

12

The sky was ablaze with stars as they pulled into the ranch. A two-story, white Victorian house with a gabled roof and dormer windows stood surrounded by manicured lawns and picket fences. Warm lights lit up the windows like eyes. The convoy pulled up and killed the engines. As the last splutter of the Jeep faded away, the door opened, letting light flood onto the porch. "Hola, mama." Gabriel hopped out of the Jeep and trotted up the stairs. In the doorway, an older woman wearing a floral print dress gasped and threw her arms out wide.

"Gabriel," she said, allowing herself to be smothered by his embrace. She pushed him back and looked at him. "Where's the cassock?"

"I'm undercover."

"Again?"

"Mama..."

The woman laughed. "Stop taking everything I say so seriously. It's good to see you. It's always good to see you." She looked at the motley crew standing by the vehicles. "And you've brought company."

"These are my friends. You know Beck. This is Carver, Velasquez, and Kip." Gabriel pointed at them one at a time. "Guys, this is my mama, Maria. You take your shoes off, you don't cuss, you don't take the Lord's name in vain, and you don't ever criticize her cooking." He looked at her. "Got room at the table for some tired reprobates?"

"Always. And beds." She looked at Kip. "You look terrible. Rough day?"

Kip nodded and smiled. "You could say that ma'am."

Maria laughed. "Let's make sure it ends on a good note with some hot food, then, huh?" She beckoned them all inside. "Come on in. Your father is in the study. Go tell him you're here and we have guests and to get his fat ass out of that chair. God forgive me." Maria crossed herself rapidly. "Miss Velasquez, you can help me set the table."

"A pleasure, Mama Monteyo." Velasquez grinned happily and trotted up the stairs.

As Beck walked past Maria, the older woman laid a hand on her arm. "Everything okay?"

Beck smiled at her. "It's a long story. Later maybe."

13

The table was littered with empty plates, bowls, and glasses. "Mama Monteyo, that was beyond amazing, as always." Beck sat back and patted her stomach.

Maria smiled warmly. "Glad you enjoyed it." She glanced at Kip and then caught Gabriel's eye. "Help mama clear the table, will you?" She scooped up an armful of tableware and headed into the kitchen.

Gabriel stood and stacked plates. "You guys chill for five." He followed his mother into the kitchen and softly closed the door.

"Mama? I know that look."

Maria scowled at her son. "This is no camping trip, is it?"

"I didn't say it was." Gabriel immediately regretted the comment as Maria's dishcloth connected with the back of his head. "Ow."

"What, you think you're too big for me to punish, now? Or do you think that because you're a monk now only God can do that?" She slapped the dishcloth down. "You're lying to me. And that disturbs me."

"Is this another of your premonitions?"

"Don't you mock me. Remember the night you almost died in Iraq? I knew then. I know now. Something is wrong." She picked the dishcloth up again and started furiously washing the dirty plates.

"I know, mama. God woke you up so you could pray for me."

"And here you are, safe and well." Maria's frown changed to a look of concern. "Something is badly wrong with your friend Kip. He seems... empty. Like his soul is missing. It's all over him. It's like Grandma used to say, 'Donde el diablo puso la mano, queda huella para rato.' Where the devil puts his hand, he leaves a mark." She watched as her son tried to keep a lid on his emotions. "I'm right, aren't I? And don't you lie to me again."

Gabriel pulled out a chair from the kitchen table and sat down. "Okay, yes. Look, we helped him get away from some very bad people."

Maria put one hand on her hip and the other on the sink drainer. "And why is that for you to do?"

Gabriel knew it was no use trying to hide anything from her. The Gift ran strong in her family and while she suppressed it as much as she could with countless Hail Marys and weekly confessionals, it was still a part of her. He sighed. "Because the same people who did bad things to Kip have Cathy. He's promised to help us find her."

Maria turned and leaned against the drainer. She spoke quietly. "Something is after him. Something evil."

"Nobody followed us, mama."

"I'm not talking about people."

"Then say extra prayers for us until we leave tomorrow, okay?" Gabriel stood and put an arm around his mother's shoulders. "Mama, we'll be fine. Really."

Maria looked at him. "Don't go with them. There's a darkness around that man. He cannot escape it. Please. I'm begging you, don't go."

Gabriel shook his head. "I have to. Beck saved my life."

Maria looked furious. "God saved your life."

The kitchen door swung open, and Beck walked in with the rest of the dishes. "Actually, the medics saved his life." She held the dishes out. "Where do you want these?"

Maria glared at Beck. "I don't care." She hurled the dish-cloth down and pushed past Beck into the dining room.

Beck watched her go and turned to Gabriel. "Everything okay?"

Gabriel stared at the door as it swung back and forth. "It will be." He looked at Beck. "Bad comment. You know how she feels."

"I think the doctors who pulled your ass out of a sling deserve a mention, is all." Beck put the plates down. "I'm gonna get the gear." She turned on her heels and stalked out of the kitchen, leaving Gabriel staring at a table full of dirty dishes and a pile of unanswered questions.

14

"Did your mom really do this all herself?" Kip stared at an exquisitely worked tapestry version of Da Vinci's Last Supper. The detailing on Christ's face was almost life-like, a tribute to the original and then some.

"Yep. She did the local church's altar cloth, too." Gabriel tapped at a laptop and then glanced up. "You guys with me here?"

"Yeah, sorry, man." Kip refocused onto Gabriel, ignoring Beck's intense gaze boring into the side of his skull.

"So here's the thing." Gabriel scanned the screen. "During the Middle Ages, several books appeared that described Hell in military terms. The devil as the commander-in-chief of seventy-two demon generals. A real chain of command kinda thing. Now, most of these books were written by religious men with good intentions." He glanced up. "And we all know what the road to Hell is paved with, don't we?"

"Good intentions." Carver piped up.

"Exactly. They wanted these books to help people like us fight evil. The things ordinary people don't want to think about, don't want to face. But someone has to step up to the plate, and it's real helpful if you have a manual or two to help you kick Satan's ass, right?" Gabriel tapped the laptop a couple of times and then spun it around. "Trouble was, some people figured out you could use these books for the opposite. As guides for summoning the very things our ancestors were trying to put back in the ground. They used them to call up demons. And Malphas is one of the generals they really latched onto in a big way."

Velasquez squinted at the laptop. "This guy?"

On the screen was a wood-carving rendition of Malphas. The black, menacing face of a raven stared out of the screen. Sweeping black wings curved upwards, like the darkest set of angel's wings. The demon had a human body, heavily muscled, and powerfully set. In one hand, he held a long, gnarled staff topped with a jagged crystal that emitted bolts of lightning. The other hand was raised in the traditional satanic salute. Beneath the clawed feet lay crushed bones and the skulls of the damned.

Even though they all knew it was an internet image of a

medieval woodcarving, the team shifted uncomfortably as the piercing eyes gazed into their souls.

Kip looked particularly upset. "You saying that thing was inside of me?"

Gabriel shook his head. "This is the thing in charge of the thing that was inside of you."

"Well that's a little reassuring. I guess." Kip still looked spooked.

Beck rallied, buried her initial reaction deep, and glared. "I know we've seen some weird shit today, and this isn't our first rodeo with the Legion. But—and I say this with the greatest respect—seriously?" She looked at Gabriel. "We're dealing with a fucking birdman?"

"Do you want my help or not?" A note of irritation snapped like a rubber band in Gabriel's voice.

"Of course I do. You know I do."

"Then trust me, okay?" The irritation softened into a gentle rebuke. "This is my field. It's why the monastery took me in. Me and Malphas?" Gabriel crossed his fingers and held them up. "We're like that. Metaphorically speaking, that is. This whole thing has his feathers all over it. And don't underestimate him. Maybe he doesn't have the same high-profile PR team as Lucifer or Baal, but he's the real deal."

Beck settled back into the couch and folded her arms. Her voice took on a practical tone. "Okay, so how? And more importantly, how do we stop him?"

Gabriel spun the laptop back and closed the lid. "Most theories of possession say the host has to allow the demon in. To embrace it, even. It's a symbiotic relationship."

"A bit like vampires having to be invited into your home,

right?" Velasquez had been happily peeling an orange. She stopped and looked up.

"Well, yes, but these ain't vamps." Carver swiped the orange out of Velasquez's hand, split it in two, and returned half to her.

"Hey."

Carver grinned. "Baby-girl, we all know that vampires are your specialty, but in this instance, we should bow to Gabe's superior knowledge, don't you think?"

"Sure. But take my orange again and I'll introduce you to Woody and stake the ever-loving crap outta you, got it?" Velasquez gave Carver a glare, who responded with a cheeky wink as he popped a segment of orange into his mouth.

"Guys?" Gabriel raised an eyebrow.

"Sorry." Velasquez and Carver both apologized together.

"Right then." Gabriel turned to Kip. "You told me the last thing you remember was some kind of baptism, right?"

Kip gulped and nodded.

"That was probably the point where Malphas inserted your passenger. Only you didn't understand what was happening, or what you were agreeing to. Demons are clever like that."

"Is he gonna hurl?" Velasquez studied the ashen-faced Kip. "Looks like he's gonna hurl."

Kip ignored Velasquez and stood up. He paced to the window and stared into the darkness. "No. I can't do this." He ran his hand through his hair and spun around. "I need some sleep. This is too much to process right now, okay? I need some sleep." He stalked out of the room, a dark cast clouding his eyes.

Beck started to go after him, but Gabriel stopped her with a gentle hand on her arm. "He's had one hell of a day. Literally. An exorcism ain't a party. I'm surprised he's still able to function, to be fair." Gabriel looked at Beck. "He needs to rest."

Beck nodded. "Malphas. He's put one of those things in Cathy, hasn't he?"

"Probably," Gabriel said, his grip tightening on her arm. "And when we find her, I promise you with every fiber of my being, I'll get it out of her. You have my word."

Carver glanced at Velasquez, who wordlessly shook her head. This wasn't the time for good-natured banter. A little girl's soul was at stake. Possibly a whole lot more, too.

Outside, the silvery light of a nearly full waxing moon glinted off the white picket fence. The house and barn looked like cut-outs made of blue paper. A soft breeze rustled the leaves in the olive grove, hissing quietly like snakes.

And in the distance, the caw of a raven cut through the night air.

15

The house fell quiet. Kip wasn't the only one who needed some rest. In the master bedroom, Jesús lay flat on his back, snoring quietly. Next to him, Maria sat still, her eyes closed and a set of rosary beads running through her fingers. Her lips moved rapidly, the words of her prayer the faintest of whispers.

In the guest bedroom, Carver lay on his stomach, taking up

most of the double bed. Gabriel had cocooned himself in woolen blankets on the fold-out cot and was finally sleeping.

And in the spare room, Velasquez was happily snoring away. Beck, however, was eyes wide open, staring through the open doorway at the closed door of the back room across the hall. Every nerve was on edge, jangling, burning. Her instincts were screaming. She was sure they'd missed something.

In the back room, Kip lay on a couch, a blanket kicked onto the floor and a pillow squeezing its way out from behind his head like a marshmallow.

A barely audible click made his eyes snap open. A second click and Kip sat bolt upright, staring at the drapes. They billowed gently, as if beckoning him. He stalked silently to the open window, wrenching the drapes apart.

In the yard, wearing white jeans and a blue polo, stood a young woman. She smiled sweetly at him. "Kip. Praise be to God. We've been so worried."

"Bobbi?"

Bobbi kept her smile fixed in place. "We've been looking everywhere for you."

"How did you find me?"

Her smile turned coy. "It wasn't easy." She gave a bell-like laugh. "But God looks after his own, and here I am. I've come to take you back. So come on. The others are waiting." The tinkling voice had a band of steel running through it. Bobbi wasn't going anywhere without Kip, that much was obvious.

Kip frowned, then motioned to her. "Wait there. I'll be right out." He turned from the window, sat on the bed and quickly put on his boots. He tried to keep things as quiet as a mouse— the last thing he wanted to do was wake the others, especially that crazy Beck woman.

In the spare room, Beck watched shadows flit back and forth, causing the light underneath the door to flicker and strobe. Her eyes narrowed. Kip was kinda restless in there for someone who claimed he needed all the rest he could get.

She heard the soft click of the door as it opened, and immediately dropped her head to the pillow, pretending to be asleep. She narrowed her eyes to slits, watching through her lashes as Kip stalked down the hallway.

Kip paused by her open doorway and looked in, checking that the two women were sound asleep.

Beck held her breath as Velasquez picked that exact moment to grunt, snort, and roll over on the bed.

Kip froze.

For what seemed like an eternity, he watched Beck's rhythmic breathing and waited for Velasquez to settle once again. Velasquez muttered something unintelligible, burrowed her face into the pillow and started to snore gently again.

Kip let out a sigh of relief and crept on past the doorway.

The second he was out of sight, Beck's eyes snapped open, and she reached under the pillow. As her hand slid out, a matte black HK45 sat cradled in her fingers. She jettisoned the mag, checked it, reinserted it, slid back the breech and flipped the safety catch to the off position. She sat upright, and swung her legs around, her feet sliding straight into her boots.

Velasquez's eyes opened. "I heard you lock and load. Everything okay?" She kept her voice to a whisper.

Beck held her finger to her lips and pointed at the open door. Velasquez nodded and silently threw the bed covers back, her own Glock 9mm already in her hand.

16

Outside the farmhouse, Bobbi waited nervously, glancing every few seconds at the branches of an old, dead tree. The black shape of a large bird sat hunched on a broken bough. The bird cawed softly. Bobbi nodded and refocused on the farmhouse door, fixing the smile back into position as the door opened.

Kip slipped out quietly, silhouetted against the soft light of the hallway. He trotted down the porch steps towards Bobbi.

She laughed and ran towards him, throwing her arms around him and hugging him tightly. "Oh, Kip." Her embrace was surprisingly strong for such a slight woman. She nuzzled her face into his neck. "They didn't hurt you, did they?"

Kip shook his head. "No, I'm fine." He returned her embrace, but with a little less enthusiasm—enough to keep her from sensing anything was wrong.

Bobbi kissed him on the cheek and smiled. "Praise God. Come on. We have to go. Now."

Kip shook his head. "I can't do that. I'm sorry."

Bobbi's smile stayed fixed, but her eyes betrayed her. "We have to. We'll die if we aren't on the mountain when the fire comes. We'll die." The lightness from her voice dissolved away.

"Pastor Reid lied to us. There's no angel. What he saw was a demon. Do you understand?"

"Is that what they told you?" Bobbi nodded towards the house. "Is that what they made you believe?"

"I don't have to believe it. I know it's true. The baptism isn't in the name of God. It's some kind of demonic possession ceremony. You have to let them in. And I did. I let one in. But it's okay because they got it out of me." He smiled gently at her.

Bobbi dropped her head onto her chest. "Oh. I see." Her voice was flat. "So they got the demon out of you, did they?"

"Yes, they did."

Her head snapped up. Her gentle blue eyes became black pits, filled with the writhing and screaming faces of the damned. "Then you better have another one." Bobbi clamped her hands on either side of his head and pulled him towards her. Her lips locked onto his mouth, and she forced her tongue into him, choking Kip as it wound down his throat. He struggled to pull away, but her grip was too strong. Black vapor swirled and curled around them, streaming in ribbons towards his nose, eyes, and mouth, probing and stabbing at him like angry snakes.

"NO."

The shout was enough to distract Bobbi for a split second. Kip wrenched himself free and stumbled to one side, landing on his ass, then pushing himself back from the possessed woman.

Bobbi roared, the sound filling the night sky and sending a flock of crows circling and reeling into the air, cawing, and squawking. A single black bird took flight from the top of the old tree, cawing angrily and swooping above Bobbi.

Beck held the gun steady. "Back off, bitch."

Bobbi's eyes went from black pits to flaming coals. She turned her attention to Kip, who scrabbled in the dirt, trying to put some distance between them. Bobbi stalked towards him, her hands flexing and cracking as her fingers elongated into claws.

"I said, back the FUCK off." Beck fired a warning shot at Bobbi's feet. "Don't make me hurt you."

Behind Beck, Velasquez assumed a covering position. "Kip. Move your ass." Velasquez yelled. "Gabriel. On us. NOW."

Bobbi ignored Beck's warning shot and reached towards Kip. Beck braced and fired two double-taps, hitting the woman in the chest. Instead of dropping lifeless to the ground, she burst into four shadows that howled in unison like a pack of wolves as they ran toward the orchard.

Beck and Velasquez opened fire at the shadows and didn't stop shooting until both of their guns were empty. Even then, Beck squeezed the trigger a few more times, her HK45 clicking uselessly.

Gabriel dashed off the porch, closely followed by Carver. "What the fuck are you shooting at?"

"The devil." Beck ran to the Jeep and ripped open her kit bag. She jettisoned the empty mag and loaded a fresh one into the pistol. She hoisted the bag onto her shoulder and ran back. "Velasquez, get him inside." She nodded to Kip, staring and hyperventilating. She dropped the kitbag and pulled out an M4. "Carver. With me." She tossed the M4 to Carver, who caught it with one hand and immediately pulled back the breech lock, flipping the safety switch off.

"Velasquez, Kip may have been compromised. Lock him down. Put him out if necessary. But don't kill him unless you absolutely have to. I need intel and I don't think he's told us everything he knows." Beck helped Velasquez haul the distraught Kip to his feet. "Go." Velasquez nodded curtly and hauled Kip towards the house.

Beck turned to the kit bag and pulled out a Glock 9mm. She held it to Gabriel.

He shook his head. "I told you. I'm not touching a gun. Ever again."

"Fine." Beck stuffed the Glock into her belt and threw a flashlight at him. "Then use this and point it at anything that looks like a mother-fucking hellhound and show us where to shoot, okay?" Beck strapped a night-vision optical unit to her skull. "Let's move." Beck, Carver, and Gabriel headed into the grove.

As she pushed Kip through the doorway, Velasquez looked over her shoulder. She watched her three friends head into the darkness. And above them, a huge black bird circled and followed them into the trees.

17

Velasquez pushed Kip through the living room door and onto the couch. "Sit. Stay." She shut and bolted the windows, then closed the drapes.

She faced Kip and leaned over him. "Look at me." Kip stared, terrified, into Velasquez's eyes. "Okay. Not seeing any hoodoo voodoo shit going on. You move, you start going all black-eyed on me, you even think of anything remotely demon-y and I'll hog-tie your ass like a little piggy, you copy?"

Kip gulped and nodded. "Copy."

"Adda boy." Velasquez pushed her Glock into her belt and turned as Maria and Jesús stumbled into the living room.

Maria looked at Kip. "I knew this would happen." She focused on Velasquez. "Where's my Gabriel?"

Velasquez's eyes narrowed. "Hunting hellhounds."

18

G abriel's flashlight punched through the dark, dancing in between the trees like a firefly on steroids. Carver kept his eyes on the beam, tracing the potential line of fire along its trajectory. He muttered quietly. "So let me get this straight. First they were people."

"Yup." Beck had her Glock held out in front of her and was doing short sweeps as she cat-stepped through the bush. "Only one. A woman. Full on *Little House on the Prairie* bitch. All plaits and freckles. Then there were six hellhounds and no sign of Freckles anywhere."

"Anyone ever tell you you've got a real way with words?" Carver grinned in the darkness. Beck's sassy nature had always been a big part of her appeal. It's what endeared her to hard-assed soldiers like Carver and Gabriel. It's why they followed her. Why they trusted her. Behind that sass was a razor-sharp strategic mind, a willingness to throw the occasional Hail Mary, when necessary, but without all the usual bravado, chick-with-something-to-prove bullshit that was such a fucking cliché. Beck was Beck. And Carver would follow her to the gates of Hell itself if she asked him to.

And they had.

Twice.

"Dogs." Carver frowned.

"Yup. But not cute little daxies." Beck gave Carver a look that suggested demonic dachshunds were not to be taken lightly.

He chuckled. "Hellhound dachshunds is something I'd wanna see. From a distance, anyway." Carver grinned as he did another sweep with the nose of his M4.

Gabriel held a fist up and they all stopped. He crouched, brushing at the ground with his fingertips, the beam of his flashlight focused on a single spot. "Hooves. Cloven."

"Deer?"

"Pigs, more likely." Gabriel stood, brushed the dirt off his fingers on his chinos.

"So not dachshunds, then?"

Gabriel turned to Carver with a puzzled look. "What?"

"Oh, nothing. You want me to?" He nodded at the M4.

"If you wouldn't mind putting your eye to that scope of yours and checking to the left of those bushes, that would be great."

Carver hoisted the M4 into position, the stock pressed hard into his shoulder, and clicked the scope on. "Dude, wanna knock that flashlight out? I've only got two retinas and one's still a bit fucked from the foxhole flashbang in Kandahar."

Gabriel muttered a quick apology and killed the light. Carver trained the M4's business end towards the track. The fluorescent green landscape though the scope was pin sharp but alien. A sudden blur flashed across the image and Carver instinctively flinched.

"What is it?" Beck's voice was a sharp rasp.

"Fucking Bigfoot, for all I know."

"Keep looking."

Carver gathered himself, adjusted the position of the M4's butt on his shoulder and kept scanning. "Nothing. Whatever that was, it's gone." He lowered the rifle. "It was fast. Damn fast." There was no question he had seen something, and to Beck's credit, she didn't do what most people would in that situation and ask Carver if he was sure he saw something. If he said something was out there, they all accepted that it was. That was the level of trust in the team. Shadows were not mere flights of fancy or figments of the imagination. They were real motherfuckers. Usually with fangs, talons, and glowing red eyes.

"We better get to the house. Velasquez is by her lonesome. And if we've got four hellhounds out here, we need to regroup rather than stumbling around in the dark." Gabriel clicked the flashlight on.

"You're right." Beck gave the blackness one last stare, challenging it silently to do its worst. "Lead on."

The three hunters headed to the house.

Behind them, four sets of burning eyes watched them go, keeping station silently, placing their paws where no crackling of a twig or rustling of a leaf would give them away.

19

Ensconced in the house's living room and using the wall as cover, Velasquez kept watch. Staring through the window, she could see almost all the porch, save one blind spot, but there was nothing she could do to cover the entire approach.

Not having a one-eighty visual annoyed the ex-sniper. She could blow the balls off a mosquito at five hundred yards. But only if she had a clean shot on the bastard. Sure, she'd taken out a Taliban chieftain straight through the open windows of a Toyota Hilux once, but there had been more than an ounce and a half of luck in that shot.

Out of the gloom came a figure. Velasquez's finger twitched next to the trigger guard, ready to take up a kill-shot stance in a nanosecond.

A dancing beam of light made her relax. Last time she heard, hellhounds didn't carry flashlights. Gabriel gave the signal and she moved quickly and opened the door. "Where's the other two?"

"Doing one last perimeter check. Kip?"

"Upstairs with your folks."

Gabriel nodded. "Lock up and keep watch."

"For what?"

Gabriel gave her a look. "For anything that isn't Beck or Carver?"

Velasquez sighed and rubbed her face. "Sorry. Been a while since I slept. Punchy, I guess."

"Then snap out of it. We've got prowlers out there and you know how smart those demon doggies can be."

"I'm good."

Gabriel gave Velasquez a gentle smile and patted her shoulder. "I know. Eyes on, okay?" He smiled one more time and stalked out of the room.

"Eyes on." Velasquez muttered to herself, slammed the deadbolt into position, and took up her watch station again. She stared into the darkness, willing Beck and Carver to appear. "Where the hell are you?" She squinted as three figures loomed out of the darkness.

Beck.

Carver.

Gabriel.

"Jesus." Velasquez sprinted to the door, threw the deadbolt back and practically wrenched the door off its hinges.

"Where's the fire?" Carver gave Velasquez a puzzled grin.

"Upstairs," Velasquez said as she sprinted after the other Gabriel.

20

He moved silently through the house and into his mom's sewing room. It had a wonderfully homey, comfortable feel, filled with memories. They weren't his memories, but there was an awareness of them at the back of his skull. He knew where to look.

Kip, Maria and Jesús watched the man they thought was

Gabriel stalk into the room. Maria's eyes narrowed. There was something off about him. "Gabriel? Is everything all right?"

He ignored her and started pawing through her knitting bag.

"What are you looking for?"

He reached into the bag, and pulled out a thick, pointed knitting needle. He studied it and smiled. "This." He turned around, the knitting needle in his hand.

Maria scowled. "What for?"

His smile widened. "For this."

He lunged forward, aiming the needle at Kip's neck. In a split second, Jesús parried the lunge away and the needle buried itself into the cushion, punching through the cloth like paper. Jesús yelled at Kip. "GO. GET OUT."

Kip ducked underneath Gabriel's outstretched arm, narrowly avoiding grasping, slashing fingers, and rolled. He sprung up and sprinted for the door. Gabriel's head swiveled like a demented owl. He watched his prey trying to flee. His hand scrabbled towards the knitting needle, and he jerked it free. Jesús threw his arms around something that looked exactly like his son, but quite clearly wasn't. He body-slammed the imposter to the ground. The sewing table sprung up in the air, scattering contents across the room. Maria screeched and scrabbled out of the way as her husband and son wrestled on the floor.

Velasquez appeared at the doorway, grabbed Kip by the collar and hauled him out of the way, hurling him into a corner of the room. "MOVE." She brought the M4 up and aimed. "Maria. Get down."

Maria hit the floor and wriggled out of the way.

Velasquez ignored Maria, steadied her breathing, and

shifted her finger from the trigger guard to the trigger. "Show me your eyes."

Gabriel stopped his Jujitsu battle with Jesús and stared at Velasquez. A guttural voice came from within her head. "Do you see them, child? Do you see the eyes of Hell? Do you see the Fire on the Mountain? Do you? DO YOU?"

Velasquez felt all the strength drain from her body, as if it were being sucked out by that stare. Her peripheral vision blurred and darkened, and the M4 shook in her hands. A black fog swirled around her, fingers of smoke probing at the corners of her eyes and her nostrils. A sharp pain jerked her back into the room. She looked down at her arm, a line of blood marking where Kip had jabbed a pair of scissors.

"Sorry... I thought—" Kip looked terrified, and the bloody scissors shook in his hand.

She gave him a quick nod, and refocused on Gabriel, this time avoiding that hellish stare. "Time for night-nights, mother-fucker." She raised the gun, but Gabriel had other ideas.

He arched his back, his head almost touching his feet, and then flipped up, grabbing Jesús by the neck with one hand and positioning the choking, kicking man in front of him like a shield. A slow, menacing smile spread across his face as he stared at Velasquez.

"DAMN IT." Velasquez didn't have a clean shot. There was the whole shooting-through-Jesús'-shoulder-to-hit-Gabriel option, but that was a shitty Hollywood movie trick and didn't fucking work in the real world. Too many arteries, too many opportunities to hit a lung and watch Jesús drown in his own blood.

No kill.

No fucking kill.

Velasquez wrestled with the agony of being armed to the teeth and unable to do a damn thing as she watched whatever the hell that thing was choke the life out of Jesús. She could see the man's eyes start to lose focus and his tongue protrude through his open mouth. He had a few more seconds at most.

As Jesús started to lose consciousness, Gabriel tossed him aside. Velasquez immediately reacted and her finger found the trigger. Before she could take the shot, Gabriel's arm shot out as if it were spring-loaded. No human could move that fast. No one. His fingers wrapped around the barrel of the M4, and he jerked the rifle out of her hands with a ferocity that sent her staggering back. His arm retracted with the rifle, he spun it around, and Velasquez found herself staring down the business end of her own rifle.

Gabriel gave her a little smile, and he wagged a finger at her. "No. Not you." He chuckled, and slowly shifted the gun's position around to Kip. "What was it you said?" Gabriel chuckled again. "Oh, that's right, nighty-night."

"NO." Carver vaulted over the prone Kip and crashed into the grinning Gabriel, slamming him to the floor. He pushed himself up, ready to start punching, if necessary, to come face to face with—

"Velasquez?"

Carver stared at his partner. "What the fu—"

"Kiss me."

"What?"

"KISS ME." Velasquez grabbed Carver on either side of his head and pulled him with surprising force down towards her. She locked her lips onto his and he felt his mouth being forced open wider and wider until he thought his jaw would snap clean from his skull. Searing pain shot through his body and he felt his throat fill with what tasted like ashes.

Velasquez's body distorted, squirmed, and started to elongate into a ribbon of smoke. The smoke, thick, black, and acrid, poured into Carver's mouth and down his throat until the last wisp vanished, leaving Carver coughing and choking on all fours.

Beck, the real Velasquez, and the real Gabriel reached the doorway in time to see Carver stop choking, and slowly stand up, a blackness in his eyes and a snarling smile pulling at the corner of his mouth. He flexed his fingers and studied them, as if he were seeing them for the first time.

Velasquez pointed. "You were right there."

Kip looked utterly baffled. "But... you, you were there too." He pointed at Velasquez.

"What the hell are you talking about?" Velasquez scowled at Kip.

"Shifters." Gabriel swore. "I hate shifters."

Kip pointed at Carver who continued to study his hand, turning it around and examining every angle. "It's inside him now."

Beck snarled. "Velasquez get mom and pop outta here. Demon Carver and I need to have a little chat."

Gabriel moved aside as Velasquez got Maria and Jesús out of the room. Maria gave Gabriel a desperate look. He nodded. "It's me, momma. It's really me."

Maria frantically crossed herself and let Velasquez herd her gently out of the room.

"Shut the door." Beck's voice had a this-is-not-open-for-debate tone.

Kip scrambled to his feet and as he moved, Carver's attention snapped away from his hand to the battered and bruised man. That slow, poisonous smile spread across his lips again and he stepped towards Kip.

Gabriel clicked the door shut.

Carver's gaze swiveled towards Gabriel. The demons inside were using Carver's military training to anticipate the next move. Now the exit point was blocked. Time to get serious. The snarling smile vanished like mist and Carver targeted Kip once again. The others could be dealt with later.

"Move and you die." Beck's voice. Her gun pointed at one of her oldest friends. It wasn't an experience she thought she'd ever repeat.

Carver stopped and turned. For a split second, the blackness in his eyes faded and Carver's soft brown orbs appeared again, filled with agony and fear. "Please, help me. I'll kill you all if you don't do something."

Gabriel held a hand out. "Hang in there."

Carver's brown eyes disappeared behind a molten blackness that swirled and twisted. He whispered. "I can't."

The M4, that had been lying unnoticed on the floor, was just a fingertip away. Carver scooped the rifle up and rolled, swinging the barrel towards Kip. He snarled. "Now, then. Where were we, you treacherous little spawn?"

Beck's boot scraped its way down Carver's shin and she shoulder-barged into him, forcing his grip to shift on the gun and sending the barrel upwards. The bullet that would've had Kip's name on it buried itself in the ceiling. Beck had just enough time to muse that Maria would be pretty pissed about that.

Her knee connected with Carver's gut, doubling the man up. As he whoofed the air out of his lungs and bent forward, Beck swung her knee into Carver's face. "Sorry." He toppled forward and she half-turned behind him and swooped his legs from under him. As he hit the floor face first, she dropped her left knee onto Carver's neck and wrenched his arm into a savage wristlock that ground bone against bone. She rolled over the top of him, twisting his spine and wrapping her legs around his arm in a harsh, unbreakable arm-lock.

"A little fucking help here." She struggled to hold the demon-possessed Carver still.

Velasquez burst through the door, gun trained on Carver. "Get that damn thing out of him before he kills us all."

"Not yet."

"I can't hold him." Beck struggled to hold Carver. The possessed man contorted and twisted, his limbs started to thrash, and he burst free of Beck's grip, vaulting to his feet, grabbing her by the ankle and swinging her like a hammer. He let go and Beck slammed into Gabriel and Velasquez, sending them all sprawling. He stood over them, the snarl-smile dripping venomous intent and malice.

Then his gaze changed. A surprised look spread over his face, he dropped to his knees and slowly toppled forward.

Behind him stood Kip, holding Maria's sewing machine. "I'm sorry. It was the closest heavy thing. He was going to kill you."

Gabriel struggled to his feet and gently took the sewing machine out of Kip's hands. "It's okay." He glanced down as Beck checked Carver's pulse. "He still with us?"

"Yeah, but man alive, is he ever gonna have one hell of a headache when he wakes up."

"Sewing-machine-induced concussion is the least of his worries, trust me." Gabriel ran his hand through his hair and puffed. "I've missed this." He sniffed. "Okay. Let's get him to the barn. We can keep him restrained there without the need to conk him with any more heavy objects, okay?"

Beck held out a hand and pulled Velasquez to her feet. Velasquez looked shaken to her core. "Okay. Can I just check something here?"

"What's that?" Gabriel smiled kindly at her.

"I'm me, you're you, and Beck is Beck, right?"

"Right."

"Cool. Just playing mental catch up." Velasquez patted herself up and down. "Yeah, I feel real. Now, give me that M4. I swear by the gods that the next fucker who isn't who they should be gets shot in the motherfucking ass."

Beck grinned. "Fair enough."

Velasquez flicked the safety catch on the M4 carbine, hoisted it to her shoulder and sniffed. "This has not been a fun evening."

Gabriel sighed. "I have a feeling it's about to get a whole lot worse."

21

The barn was cold, dark, and smelled of sweet hay, acrid horse urine, and rusty iron.

The iron would help.

Demons hated iron.

It bent their world out of shape. It twisted and distorted things, making the demonic realm squirm and writhe.

It also burned. Burned like a motherfucker. Iron was older than Hell. Much, much older. It had ancient, raw, elemental magic in every molecule, magic that even demons couldn't battle. Magic that went to the very beginning of Time.

Beck knew that. Which was why Carver was currently wrapped in enough rusty iron chains to hold Lucifer himself. The fact that he was hanging upside down five feet off the ground would probably also make getting free considerably more difficult.

Beck's heart was aching. Carver was one of her oldest friends. More than that, he was her oppo. He'd been there, in foxhole after foxhole with tracers stuttering over the tops of their heads, the Taliban just yards away, screaming about what they were going to do to them when they got to them. He'd been there when the bullet with her name it on finally found its mark. He'd been in the Chinook with her as the medics fought like hell to stop her from bleeding out.

He'd always been there.

He was a part of her. He was her brother in arms.

And she'd repaid him by wrapping him in chains and hanging him from a hook in a barn.

This was gonna take more than an apology and a shitload of beers to expunge.

She watched as Gabriel, rosary wrapped around his right hand and open Bible in his left, read the words quietly. She knew how much pain Carver was in. The touch of so much iron would be almost unbearable by now.

The ancient iron magic was doing its work. The demons who currently used Carver as a corporeal Uber were struggling to keep control. The holy words tumbling from Gabriel's mouth were also shifting the reality for the denizens. Carver kept asserting control, if only briefly.

For a second, Carver came back. "Help me. It hurts."

"You can do this. I know you can. You're stronger than they are." Gabriel's voice was soft, reassuring.

The response came not from Carver, but from a Legion buried within his soul. They could be seen, just beneath his skin. His body writhed and twisted as demon after demon tried to assert dominance, battling with Carver for control. Carver roared and thrashed, convulsing, and rattling the chains like Marley's ghost on speed. "NO."

A chorus of voices roared in unison. "HE IS WEAK. PATHETIC. HIS SOUL IS OURS. THE MOUNTAIN WILL BURN."

"Where are you?" Gabriel circled Carver. "Tell me where the mountain is."

"WE WILL NEVER TELL YOU."

"Why?" Gabriel kept his voice soft, gentle, a reactionary barrier to the vitriol and hate wrapped up in that chorus of Hell. "Because you're scared, aren't you?" He continued to circle the thrashing Carver. "You're starting to lose your certainty of the Burning, aren't you? We're close, aren't we?"

"NO. NO."

"What's it like to feel fear, demons? To feel something you instill in others. That you use with such casual disdain. What's it like, demons?" Gabriel turned the screw tighter. Carver thrashed and screamed. Then—

"Mommy?"

A child's voice replaced the hellish chorus. A sweet, timid voice. All blue eyes and curls. All smiles and kisses.

Beck felt her world implode. "Cathy? Baby? Is that you?"

Gabriel spun around. "No. It's not Cathy. You hear me? It's not Cathy."

Cathy's voice filled the barn. "You're hurting me, mommy. I'm scared."

Gabriel stood between Beck and the writhing Carver. "It's a trick. You know it's a trick. It's all they've got. Illusions and empty promises. Lies upon lies. It's not Cathy."

"He's a bad man, mommy." Cathy's voice took on an edge filled with needles and razor blades. "They all are. And so are you. Why are you hurting me, mommy? Why? Why do you listen to a man who thinks a robe and a rope make him wise? He's a fool, mommy." Her voice became guttural. "And so are you, mommy. You'll ALL BURN. Because you're BAD, mommy, you're bad."

Gabriel stared at Beck and shook his head. It didn't work. Beck had been taken in by the illusion, the lies of the demons.

"Don't say that baby. mommy isn't bad. I love you, Cathy. I'm coming to get you, baby girl. I'm coming to get you." Beck's legs felt like they were about to fold up underneath her.

Gabriel held out a hand, ready to catch her. "Don't listen to them."

The demons pushed the advantage. They'd found a chink in the armor. And they knew how to open that chink until it became a gaping, aching hole in Beck's heart. Cathy's voice took on a petulant tone, accusatory and harsh. "It's true. All those people you killed told me how bad you are. You're wicked, mommy. Wicked. And you're going to BURN."

Gabriel rounded on the host currently using Carver as a vessel. "Quit with the cheap shots, already." He leaned in and snarled, all illusion of priestly gentleness and turn-the-other-cheek kindness gone. "Just tell us where you are so we can come and get you."

Cathy's voice became multi-layered, flip-flopping from

guttural to shrill. The voices came from all directions at once. "Come for us, priest. Come for us. We await you and your pathetic little friends. Your blood will soak the soil. Your fat will feed the flames that will consume all. Your bones—"

"Yes, yes, we know, all manner of hellish horrors awaits us, yada, yada, yada." Gabriel interrupted the host and rolled his eyes. "Okay, then, let's see what we've got here." He took out a small bottle of holy water from a pocket and pulled the cork out with his teeth like he was opening a bottle of sipping whisky, spitting the cork across the barn. He held up the holy water. "Know what this is?" He splashed a few droplets on Carver's face, and the Legion roared. "Enough. Tell us the zip code."

"Come. Come one, come all. We await you at the Black Moon Mine, outside of Barlote. Highway 49." Carver smiled a poisonous smile. "See you there, priest."

With a wet, cracking noise, two black hands prized their way out of Carver's extended mouth, making him choke and scream in pain. Thick, black smoke poured from his mouth and took a vaguely human form. It whooshed into the eaves of the barn and the entire building was filled with an ear-shattering scream, as if a thousand souls cried out as one. Gabriel, Beck and Velasquez covered their ears and screwed their eyes shut as the scream rose in pitch and volume, until it felt like every molecule in their bodies was vibrating. The Legion, splitting into multiple black smoke figures, swooped, and spun through the air, finally erupting through the open hay window at the top of the eaves.

Then, as suddenly as it started, it stopped.

The silence was deafening.

"Will someone please get me the fuck down from here." Carver's voice sounded like a wood saw scraping across glass.

Gabriel opened one eye, peered at Carver, and launched the rest of the holy water straight into his face.

"Dude. Seriously?"

"Had to be sure." Gabriel gave Carver an apologetic look and turned to Velasquez. "Could you?"

"Already on it." Velasquez punched the button that lowered the hay trolley cable, complete with still-chained Carver, gently down to the ground. She set about the chains, opening the padlocks, and unwrapping her friend from his bonds. "You okay, big guy?"

Carver let the last of the chains fall away from him, looked at Velasquez, and gently keeled over sideways into her waiting arms.

Velasquez looked up. "He'll be okay, right?"

Gabriel nodded. "He'll hurt like hell for a few days, but he'll be fine. Take care of him" His voice was soft again, the confrontation and aggression he'd demonstrated earlier gone, buried deep for when it was needed next.

In a corner, Beck sobbed quietly. She'd been strong for so long. She'd held it together for the sake of the others. But hearing Cathy's accusations had been hard, even though she knew it wasn't her. Because if it were, that would mean—

No.

She couldn't even think that.

Somewhere, Cathy was alive. Waiting for her mommy to come get her. Waiting to run into her arms, all smiles and happy laughter. All kisses and curls.

Cathy.

Beck's heart broke.

Cathy...

She didn't feel Gabriel's arms around her, holding her tight, pulling her close. She sobbed into his jacket, unable to catch her breath and gasping with the pain that filled her soul.

Cathy...

Gabriel rocked Beck gently, smoothing a wisp of hair from her forehead and holding her tighter as the sobs wracked her again and again.

Cathy...

Outside the barn, a howl went up. The hounds, calling up the wind. Calling up the darkness. They would keep pace with their quarry to the end. Four hounds. One for Carver. One for Velasquez. One for Gabriel. One for Beck.

The howl reached a crescendo, and the last notes were taken away by a maelstrom that whipped the dust into spirals and the howl of the hellhounds to the sky.

Then, the silence came again.

The hounds faded into the darkness, their corporeal form becoming as translucent as mist, ribbons blowing through the meadow and through the olive groves.

They waited.

22

Even though Maria's living room was homey, comfortable, and full of warmth, there was a tension in the air as thick as peanut butter. Everyone was on edge. Everyone was what Velasquez liked to call "spiky." Nerves were shredded and explosions were close to the surface. It was like driving down a desert lane through Kandahar, knowing there were IEDs every few yards, but not exactly knowing when or where they'd go off.

Just like old times, then.

Beck sat, staring at a laptop screen, while Velasquez dabbed iodine onto the cuts and bruises Carver was now sporting. He winced and flinched from a particularly hard dab. "Ow."

"Oh, shut up, baby boo." Velasquez dabbed again, ignoring his protestations.

"Did you have to do those chains up so tight? I look like a pinata."

"Oh, didums. Did der bad ladies beat your ass?" Velasquez sat back, a serious look on her face. "We had no choice, big guy. You know that."

Carver gave his oppo a small smile and squeezed her hand. "I know."

All eyes turned to Gabriel as he moved silently into the doorway. Carver looked worried. "Is everyone okay up there?"

Gabriel nodded. "Dad's banged up a bit and won't be singing opera any time soon. Don't worry, he'll be fine. Mom was more interested in making sure I tell you all how right she was. I've heard 'I told you so' in Spanish and English at least fifteen times already." He slumped into a chair.

Velasquez patted Carver on the arm. "You're done." She stood and brushed her hands on her jeans. "What about Kip?"

"Scared, for sure. But he still wants to help."

"That's a joke, right?" Beck scowled. "No way. Not after tonight. I trust him as far as I could kick his ass on a windy day."

"I agree." Gabriel nodded.

"You do?" Beck sounded surprised.

"Yes."

Velasquez frowned. "Hang on a minute, if it hadn't been for Kip conking Carver with your momma's sewing machine, sorry, dude," Velasquez paused and gave Carver an apologetic look, "we'd all be smears on the floorboards right about now."

"Good point, but those shifters wouldn't have found us without him, too. That's my guess, anyway."

"That's quite a reach." Velasquez fussed at Carver's hair, checking the large lump on his skull where the sewing machine had made contact.

"Not really. Momma said she knew something was wrong from the moment she laid eyes on him. She said she could smell it on him."

Carver frowned. "He's not a meat patty that's gone bad."

"I know. But didn't you notice it? That sulfur smell? Like rotten eggs?"

"Dude, I was too busy dealing with the smoke demons trying to turn me inside out at the time to figure out what kind of deodorant they were using." Carver sounded peevish. "You think I've got this smell now? Is your momma gonna start giving me the stink-eye and squirting air freshener at me?"

Gabriel shook his head. "No, you're good. They were in you for less than an hour. They were in Kip for months. It's kinda like a viral load, you know? The more you're exposed to it, the more intense it becomes."

"I still think he wants to help." Velasquez sat on the couch and crossed her arms.

"We can't take the risk. We'll drop him where he wants before we head up the hill." Beck scribbled some numbers on a piece of paper and closed the laptop with a snap.

"How far is it?" Gabriel asked.

Beck rubbed her eyes and yawned. "About sixty miles. Place has quite a history, too. I'll tell you on the way. But right now, I'm good for nothing but sleep."

Gabriel stood up. "I think that's a good idea. We've had enough excitement for one night. See you all in the morning." He waved a hand and walked out of the room.

Carver stared at Velasquez. "Did he just give us a benediction on the fly?"

Velasquez grinned. "Force of habit, I guess."

Carver chuckled and stood, stretching his arms out carefully and arching his back. "I'm beat. Nighty night, girls."

Velasquez sighed and pushed herself out of the sofa. "You coming?"

Beck nodded. "I'll be along in a minute."

Velasquez stroked her hair. "Make sure you do. You look wasted." She smiled gently and walked out of the room, leaving Beck alone for the first time in days.

Beck frowned and stood, stalking to the window, and easing back the net curtain to stare into the darkness.

Eight pinpricks of red light stared back at her.

A soft chorus of growling, barely audible to the human ear, filled the night air.

23

The house was awake early. Maria and Jesús stood on the front steps and watched Beck load up the last of the bags into the Jeep. Velasquez and Carver humped a suspiciously heavy looking ammo box into the Mini. Gabriel stood with his parents, watching his friends.

Kip Marton, sporting a natty combination of ill-fitting chinos and a green dress shirt that was clearly meant for a much larger man, shuffled into the sunlight. He blinked and rubbed his eyes, then turned to Jesús. "Thanks again for the change of clothes, Mister Monteyo."

"De nada." Jesús smiled and patted the man on the shoulder. "I'm sure you'll grow into them eventually." He grinned and then winced, rubbing at the red welts around his neck.

Carver slammed the Mini's trunk shut and turned. "And I'm truly sorry about your sewing machine, Momma."

Maria scowled briefly before giving the big man a bright smile. "At least I know what to put on my Christmas list now, huh?"

"Let me take care of that." Beck dusted her hands on her shorts and turned to Maria.

The old woman gave Beck a hard stare. "You take care of my son, you understand?"

"You kidding? He's the one taking care of us." Velasquez wilted under Maria's stare.

Beck stepped forward. "We'll all take care of each other. After all, we couldn't do this without him. You know that." Beck's voice was soft and serious. "I'll bring him back to you." She held up her little finger. "Pinkie promise."

Maria's eyes glistened but she fought the tears back. She focused on Gabriel, and without warning, flung her arms around her son and held him tight. "Call me as soon as it's over. I'll be praying for you."

Gabriel returned the hug, his huge arms enveloping the little woman. "Thank you."

"Can I get on that list?" Beck gave Maria a little smile.

Maria gave Gabriel one last squeeze and finally let him go. She sniffed and quickly wiped her eyes, so that nobody saw the tears of fear that lined them. "Of course. I'll pray for every one of you." She smoothed her apron and sniffed again. "Now, go. Go save the world. And may God be with you."

Maria and Jesús watched as the team climbed into their cars. They didn't look away until the dust trail leading finally dissipated into the early morning breeze.

Jesús wound his fingers into Maria's hand and squeezed gently. He could feel the dread making her hand tremble. It resonated with his own dark foreboding. The bright sunshine of an early fall day couldn't burn away the darkness lurking on the edge of his consciousness.

A darkness that, if Gabriel and the team couldn't stop it, would spread across the planet like a plague and kill them all.

24

The bus station was busy with passengers all bustling and jostling. Places to be, people to see. As a snapshot of humanity swirled around them, Kip and Gabriel sat calmly on a bench in front of a wall of rental lockers. Kip stared at his hands, picking idly at a hangnail. Gabriel let his mind wander, drifting into that quiet, sacred space he went to whenever he could. A place of peace. Of serenity. A place where he could be close to God.

God, however, had different ideas, and a tap on his arm brought him back to the real world. Too loud. Too bright. Too imposing.

Beck stopped in front of them. "Well? What did your brother say?" She stared at Kip.

"'Told you so.' It's kind of his default for anything when it comes to me."

"That's gotta suck."

Kip shrugged. "He's right. And he's totally okay with having me stay with him for a few days so he can constantly remind me of the fact of how right he was and how wrong I was."

Gabriel laid a hand on Kip's shoulder. "If it's any consolation, Beck and I have made bigger mistakes than you, and we turned out reasonably okay, if a little damaged around the edges. You'll be fine."

"Hopefully." Kip went back to staring at his hands. "What time's my bus?"

Beck looked at Gabriel and raised an eyebrow. Gabriel shook his head. Kip was in a bad place right now. He didn't need Beck's notoriously brisk comebacks, just a bit of time and space to heal. Beck gave Gabriel a silent nod, then held out a ticket and a twenty-dollar bill. "Not until five. Take this and get yourself something to eat while you wait."

Kip stared at the outstretched hand and then at Beck. He looked small. Lost. Alone. "Thank you." He carefully took the ticket and the bill from Beck's hand and his head dropped again. "It's more than I deserve." He looked up. "I wish I could help more."

Beck shrugged. "I know where my little girl is, thanks to you. So that makes us even in my book."

Kip started to speak again, but Beck gave him a curt nod

that cut him off as she stalked away. Kip watched her go, and his shoulders fell. "She blames me, doesn't she?"

"No. Worse than that." Gabriel watched Beck head to a vending machine and dig in her pocket for some change. "She blames herself. And she's her own worst critic." He turned to Kip. "Don't be too harsh on yourself. None of this was your fault."

Kip shook his head. "How do I pay you back for your kindness?"

"You don't." Gabriel stood up. "There's a saying in my monastery. 'The water puts the fire out. We are merely the hose.'"

Kip looked confused. "I don't understand."

Gabriel smiled. "One day you will. Be well, Kip Marton. Go with God."

Before Kip could answer, Gabriel turned and walked away. He caught up with Beck, who had finally managed to extract a Hershey bar from the vending machine. "We ready?"

Beck pocketed the candy bar and nodded. "Let's go."

Without looking back at Kip, they walked out of the station.

Kip sat alone on the bench, forlorn, alone. All he'd wanted to do was help.

Outside, Beck and Gabriel walked across the parking lot towards the cars. Beck scowled and spoke, her voice carrying a hint of an accusation. "When you said our mistakes were bigger than his. Is that what you really think? Or were you trying to make the guy feel better about playing fuck around and find out with the Legion?"

Gabriel frowned. "We've all made mistakes, you can't deny that. I mean, what's a bigger mistake than murder?"

Beck stopped and turned to Gabriel, her eyes darkening.

"We didn't murder anyone. We killed them. In combat. Otherwise they would've killed us. Maybe something worse for Velasquez and me."

Gabriel frowned. "Is that what you really think? Or are you saying that to make yourself feel better?"

"Touché." Beck glared at her friend. "Is that what it's come to? You've finally reached that holier-than-fucking-thou level, haven't you?" She tensed. "You fucking hypocrite."

Gabriel held up a hand. "Whoa. Slow down there, firecracker. You know that's not what I said. And you know I don't blame you for a damn thing we've done over the years." His face was stony. "I wasn't always a monk."

Beck vibrated with inner rage for a few seconds, took a deep breath, and relaxed. "Yeah. I know. Sorry." She touched his arm.

Gabriel stroked her hair and shushed her. "Let's focus on Cathy. Let's get her back, stop Armageddon, again, go get some beers, and then drop me back at the monastery so I can spend the rest of my days cataloguing books and selling wine, okay?"

"Deal." Beck gave him a flicker of a smile. She looked towards the parking lot, where Velasquez and Carver stood engaged in a silent war of Rochambeau. She nodded. "Waddya think those two are fighting over?"

Gabriel laughed. "Knowing them, who gets the biggest gun." He watched as Carver threw his head back in disbelief and Velasquez punched the air, victorious with her paper over his rock. "Guessing Velasquez gets the fifty caliber, then." Gabriel grinned. "Shall we?"

The two friends walked towards their oppos.

And towards the battle to come.

25

The afternoon sun lit the blacktop and gave it a shimmering, mirage-like heat haze. The El Dorado County Line took them along Highway 50 and up into the Sierra Nevada mountains. The Jeep felt hot as a furnace.

Gabriel, lounging as comfortably as he could in the passenger seat, checked the GPS on Beck's phone. He kept one eye on the numbers, but his mind was elsewhere. Something was nagging at the back of his skull.

This was all too damn easy. Getting a personal invitation to the end of the world wasn't the usual demonic modus operandi. As he delved into his memory, Beck filled up the empty space between them with idle chatter.

"Black Moon was the biggest gold mine in the state until it was closed in 1923."

Gabriel nodded, checked the GPS, and went back to staring at the passing landscape.

"The whole thing was like, six thousand feet deep, or something." Beck glanced at Gabriel, who grunted. She frowned. "There's over three hundred miles of tunnels. Lots of them are full of water now."

"Uh-huh."

Beck's frown deepened. "Sixty-two miners died in an accident. That's why it shut down. Wanna know how they died?"

"Hmm?"

"The miners." She slapped the steering wheel. "Dude, are you with me here?"

Gabriel snapped back into the here and now. "Sorry. Guess the lack of sleep caught up with me for a bit. Where were we?"

"Miners. Dead miners. Sixty-two of them."

"Dunno. Drowned? Cave in?"

Beck shook her head. "No. Fire." She shifted down a gear as the ascent started to make the Jeep's engine struggle.

Gabriel's eyebrows raised. "As in—"

"As in the mountain that burns." Beck nodded. "I couldn't believe it either. They never found the cause. I mean, underground fires aren't exactly rare in mining, but this one was so ferocious that it melted the rockface. One rumor was the miners had dug all the way to Hell in their never-ending greed for gold and the devil had taken their souls as retribution."

Gabriel laughed. "Sounds like someone's got some great public relations going on. Tourists love a bit of brimstone and hellfire."

"Every tourist business at the mine's gone bust within six months. Prospectors looking for some legendary lost seam of gold known as Satan's Peak disappear on a regular basis. And then ten months ago the Lightbringers bought the place." She glanced at Gabriel. "I ask you. Seriously. What would a religious sect want with a mine?"

"Tourist attraction?" Gabriel shrugged. "Or perhaps a short-cut straight to Hell, if the rumors are anything to go by." He ran his hand through his hair. "About earlier..."

She interrupted him. "I'm sorry. For calling you a hypocrite. I didn't mean it." Beck's voice was clipped. Sharp.

"Of course you did. You meant every word. And, before you go off like an IED, I don't blame you." Gabriel touched her arm. "I can be sanctimonious sometimes. Even the Abbot thinks so. But know this." He looked at Beck. "I'd kick down the gates of Hell itself for you. And for Cathy."

Beck sniffed hard, forcing the tears down. "Back at you. Sorry about dragging your sanctimonious sorry ass out of that safe little monastery and actually to the gates of Hell, dick-head." Her voice softened. "And for what happened at Al-Qa'im."

"Water under the bridge." He took a deep breath. "For what it's worth, I'm sorry too."

The GPS's squawky, nasal voice cut in. "In a quarter mile, take exit forty-one for Greenstone Road."

Beck mimicked the GPS. "She's a naggy little bitch, isn't

she?" She eased the power off and clicked the turn signal on. "Right then. Miner Manor Hotel, here we come." The Jeep turned onto a blacktop that quickly deteriorated into a fire road, the surface pitted with tracks leading up to the remote hotel.

"We checking in as us?" Gabriel peered ahead, catching glimpses of the hotel's lights in the distance.

Beck gave him a dark look. "Well, we were invited by the Legion itself, so hey, why not?" She focused on the track. "There's no element of surprise in this hunt. They know we're coming, so hell, let's go in with a fanfare and all guns blazing, huh?"

Gabriel settled back in the seat and scowled. "Yeah. That's what I'm worried about."

26

The hotel had done its very best to capture that "Old Timey" vibe. Wooden slatted walls, a saloon bar door, shutters, and a daily "gunfight" with actors pretending to be shot and diving off the roof were all part of the average tourist package. The trouble was that the team currently rolling their wagons into the lot next to a suspiciously new-looking hitching post were anything but average tourists.

Beck climbed out of the Jeep and waited until Velasquez

and Carver had parked. The four looked at the hotel and exchanged glances. "I'll get us checked in. Then we'll do a daylight recon. Map out our approach for tonight."

"Copy that. Me and Carver'll check the kit. You know. Away from prying eyes." Velasquez grinned.

"Fair comment. Make sure no Chads and Barbaras get too inquisitive, okay?" Beck turned and walked towards the saloon doors.

Gabriel watched her go inside and then turned to Velasquez. "Before she gets back, fill me in on this YouTube video."

Velasquez frowned. "Total bullshit. Start to finish. Designed to do nothing except push her buttons, hard. Her ex set her up. Took her to the mall where some of the guys from the church were waiting to give her a metric shit-ton of abuse about how women shouldn't serve."

"I can imagine there was only one logical outcome to that, then?" Gabriel frowned.

"You imagine right." Carver nodded. "He knew what she'd do, how badly she'd go off. And she did." He did a "poof" hand gesture. "Like a fucking APM, man. And naturally, all his buddies were there with their cellphones on video record. Next thing, the internet's full of a crazy lady going batshit on this group of holy Joes on a church outing." He glanced at Gabriel. "No offense, man."

"None taken." Gabriel gave him a smile.

Velasquez sniffed and rubbed her nose. It was something she did when she was as mad as hell but didn't want to show it openly. Gabriel knew it was one of her tells, a tell that at least three not-so-wise men had mistaken for interest in bars across the world. It usually ended badly. "Yeah. Then that asshole went and told the judge at the next child support hearing that

Beck was like that all the time. Unstable. Unpredictable. And that her behavior was, and I quote, 'creating a dangerous environment for their daughter'. I mean, what a piece of fucking work that guy is." Velasquez glared at the ground and kicked a stone, sending it skittering across the car lot.

"Heads up." Carver nodded as Beck batted the saloon doors open, ignoring the "Take it easy lady" from the clerk inside. She took the steps two at a time.

"Fuck. I know that look." Velasquez popped the trunk of the Range Rover and lifted the false bottom, revealing an array of deadly ordnance.

Beck reached her friends. "They're in the park. Bandstand. Right now."

"Who is?"

"Father fucking Christmas, who do you think?" The filter Beck worked so hard to keep positioned between her brain and her mouth vanished. She reached into the Range Rover, grabbed a Glock, checked it, and scooped up two magazines on the run. "Move. Now. NOW."

Velasquez, Carver, and Gabriel didn't need telling twice. They moved.

27

Gold Rush Park was an attempt to depict the miserable, often short lives of gold prospectors in search of fortune and glory in a more accessible and sanitized way. Old tools littered the park, and boards with brightly colored maps and graphics charted the lives of the prospectors, minus the whole cholera, dysentery, alcoholism, and financial ruin side.

In the middle of the park, and totally out of character with rest of the whole rootin'-tootin' rustic theme was a surprisingly ornate bandstand. Victorian-style ironwork collided with genteel East Coast design, finished off with a shit-ton of Art Nouveau scrolling and floral motifs. A canopied roof kept the afternoon sunshine at bay. For decades, prospectors blessed with more enthusiasm than actual musical talent had put on shows for their comrades, rivals, and an arch enemy. The obsessive love of gold was put aside for a few hours while honky-tonk bands, hoedowns and the occasional warbly singer soothed troubled souls and gnarled, blistered hands with a tune or two.

Today, the bandstand played host to a very different form of entertainment—a diatribe designed to convince the initiated and a handful of non-believers who'd stumbled in on the meeting without warning that it was time to get their affairs in order. Pastor Thomas Reid was everything every TV evangelical wished they could be. He had the salt and pepper hair, the chiseled jaw, the piercing blue eyes, and a smile that had paid for his orthodontist's last cruise.

That smile was dazzling.

And so very, very convincing.

It was a Cheshire Cat smile that would live in the memory long after Pastor Reid had faded into nothingness.

Hanging on his every word were a crowd of about forty Lightbringers, all dressed like they were on a preppy day out from a New England high school. White jeans and dark blue polo shirts abounded. Vacant, smiling faces were upturned, soaking in Pastor Reid's every syllable. The pastor had them enraptured, even though the words were full of dread.

"It's too late. At dawn tomorrow, everything you know will

be gone." The bullhorn squeaked. He swooped his hand over the congregation. "The fire is coming. To wipe all this clean. To remove the disease of humanity. To open the gates and allow the Golden Time to begin. You. You have been called, my children. You have been called to build a better world. Your time approaches. Are you ready? Are you?"

A slight unease ruffled the crowd. Not everyone listening to Pastor Reid wore the Lightbringer uniform. A group of young people started talking among themselves and laughing. One voice let out a derogatory, "Yeah, right. Cool story, bro," causing a new ripple of laughter.

Reid stared at the hecklers. The bullhorn dropped to his side, and he spoke directly at them. His voice didn't need the advantage of a megaphone. Even from the back, Gabriel, Beck, and the team could hear him quite clearly. "Cool story? Yes it is, bro." That Cheshire Cat grin widened. "And tomorrow you'll find out how cool, my friend." He put a hand on his thigh and leaned further forward. "How's Susan, Dwayne? How's the treatment going?"

Dwayne stopped his sneering asides and stared at the preacher. "What the fuck?" His eyes narrowed. "How'd you know about—"

"About Susan? About the chemo that hasn't been working right up until today?" Reid's gaze had Dwayne locked to the spot. "Call her. Call her now. Find out what the doctors have discovered. Then?" He stood straight and spread his arms wide open. "Then come and join us and find out how you can be a part of our new world." He addressed the rest of the hecklers. "That goes for all of you, children. Join us. Or die."

Dwayne finally broke the gaze, and immediately scrabbled

for his cellphone. He moved away from his friends, talking in hushed, rapid tones.

Velasquez scowled. "You know, I think that whole join-us-or-die ending needs a little work." Carver gave Velasquez a hard dig in the ribs with his elbow. "Hey. What the fuck, big guy?" Carver nodded towards Beck, and Velasquez followed his gaze. Her voice dropped to a barely audible whisper. "Oh. Fuck."

Beck was motionless. Tears ringed her eyes, and one had the audacity to make a break for freedom by hanging momentarily on her eyelash and then tumbling down her cheek like a diamond dropped by a cat burglar.

In the grassy meadow next to the bandstand, six children were busy playing a game of tag. Their laughter tinkled across the park as they tore around, playfully teasing one another.

In the middle of the game raced a little girl, her face flushed and peals of laughter ringing from her.

All blue eyes and curls.

All smiles and kisses.

Cathy...

Gabriel put a gentle hand on Beck's shoulder. "She looks exactly like you."

Beck turned her face to Gabriel. "She does, doesn't she?" She looked back at the children as they played. "She really does."

"Where's that asshole of an ex of yours?" Velasquez scowled and scanned the crowd.

"Huh?" Beck tore her gaze away from Cathy for a second and looked around. "He's not here." She started forward. Gabriel's gentle hand turned into a hard grip.

"Where'd you think you're going?"

"Where the fuck do you think?" Beck tried to brush his

hand away. "I'm going to get her. She's right there. I can grab her, and we can get the hell out of Dodge. Velasquez, diversion." Beck started forward again, but Gabriel's hand moved quickly from her shoulder and wrapped around her arm. He hauled her backwards.

"No. You can't do that."

"Watch me."

Gabriel spoke quickly. "We grab Cathy now, the whole plan goes out the window."

"There's a plan?" Beck glared at Gabriel.

"The plan to stop them literally unleashing Hell?" Velasquez frowned. "Remember?"

"Beck, it's not only Cathy's life at stake here. It's the whole of humanity." Gabriel's grip tightened as he silently struggled with Beck. "You grab her. Then what? We'd have to fight our way out of a situation where a whole crowd of civilians could get hurt or killed. Cathy'd be scared out of her mind, and all the indoctrination they've been pumping into her head would be confirmed by 'crazy momma' kidnapping her in broad daylight." He hissed. "You wanna go to jail? I mean, obviously, if there were any jails left after the whole burning mountain Armageddon thing has finally calmed down?" He shook her arm. "We stick to the plan."

Carver moved and stood facing Beck, blocking her view of Cathy. "He's right. Listen. We're here. We're within touching distance of Cathy, I know. But we move now, we blow everything."

Beck strained, desperate to break Gabriel's grip. She snarled at Carver. "She's not your little girl. She's mine. She's my baby. And they took her from me."

"And we'll get her back." Carver bear-hugged Beck, and

Gabriel released his grip. "All of us. Together. And then we'll stop those motherfuckers from whatever hoodoo-voodoo shit they've got planned for the rest of us, okay?"

Gabriel nodded at Carver and then spoke quietly to Beck. "The best thing we can do is get clear of here before any of them recognize us."

"They already know we're coming." Velasquez was still busy scanning the crowd.

"But they don't know we're here."

"Yeah, I think you may be a little off-base there." Velasquez locked her gaze onto Pastor Reid, who was staring directly at them and smiling that Cheshire Cat smile as hard as he could. "We're busted."

Gabriel turned and looked at the pastor. The world seemed to stop. In unison, the crowd turned and stared at Beck, Gabriel, Carver and Velasquez. The pastor spoke quietly, but every word echoed around the park.

"You are not among the Chosen. You have eyes, but they are blind to the truth. You have ears, but you refuse to hear. Your souls cry out to be saved, but you ignore their pleas." The smile vanished and his eyes blackened. "The mountain will consume you." He raised his hand and extended a finger, pointing directly at Beck. "You will not stop us. The mountain will burn."

Pastor Reid dropped his hand and silence filled the park. He turned to one of the Lightbringers. "Gather the children. We have much to prepare."

"NO." Beck struggled against Carver's embrace as Cathy and the other children were shepherded away. The Lightbringers filed onto a waiting bus and the doors hissed closed.

The last thing that Beck saw through her tears was Cathy's

face on the bus, staring straight at her mom, her little hands pressed against the glass. The little girl's eyes widened, and she mouthed a single word: "Mommy?"

The bus vanished in a cloud of dust and Beck let out a wail that came from the very depth of her soul.

28

T he bed was covered with ordnance. M4 carbines lay side by side with HK45 pistols, bullet-proof vests, and low-profile headsets with boom mics. A stack of magazines and boxes of loose bullets made sure that all this hardware had plenty of stopping power. Between the two beds stood two tripods with scopes mounted to the tops. One was a 1500mm daylight. The other was a thermal. Velasquez fiddled with the scopes, making sure she was happy they were tuned in.

For her, hitting a bullseye was a matter of professional pride. Clean, quick, simple. There'd be no messy sideswipes, ricochets, or flesh wounds on her watch.

Beck, her eyes still red and her nerves still raw, shoved a cleaner down the barrel of a Glock 9mm. She glanced up and scowled. "What's wrong with you? You look like a vegetarian at a slaughter-house."

Gabriel stood staring at the weapons. "They're civilians. Is all this really necessary?"

Beck went back to cleaning the gun. "Only if they start shooting first. Then? That lot may not be enough." She put the Glock down. "Don't worry, monk. You'll be well away from the nasty bangy things, okay?"

"Don't patronize me." Gabriel frowned at her. "You could've driven past the monastery, you know."

Beck sighed. "Are we going to have this conversation again? You know, about how we need you?"

"No. But drop the passive-aggressive act."

"And?"

"Well, stick to the aggressive bit, I guess. At least that's you being honest about the situation." Gabriel turned and wandered over to the window.

Velasquez smiled a little too brightly. "Anyone got food? I'm starving."

Beck reached into a backpack and pulled out a PowerBar. She tossed it to Velasquez. "Chew on that."

Velasquez studied the bar. "Oh yay. Rocky Road." She tore the corner of the pack with her teeth and spat out the little triangle of foil wrapper. "Sadly, it does taste like blacktop."

Beck managed to raise a smile. "Gabriel? Want a piece of Route 66 with added peanuts?"

"No. That's another thing I swore I'd never touch." He turned from the window. "And of the two, you'll see me with a gun in my hand before you see me with one of those monstrosities in my mouth. Seriously Vel. How do you even?"

Velasquez chomped happily. "I kinda like 'em. Although I think that those pink bits may not actually be mini marshmallows, you know?"

"Weirdo." Carver chuckled and snatched the PowerBar out of mid-air.

"Asshole." Velasquez took another bite and grinned, chewing noisily.

Carver grinned back and ripped the top off the power bar pack. "I know, right? We're supposed to believe they got the tech to build shit that can see in the dark, but they can't make an MRE that doesn't taste like ass?"

Velasquez stopped mid-chew, a puzzled expression on her face. "How you know what ass tastes like?"

"Six years in the service."

Velasquez shrugged and grunted, taking another bite of the bar. "Copy that."

Beck pushed the fully serviced Glock into her waistband and stood. She moved to a small table where a topographical map of the region filled the screen of her laptop. "Okay. Get close and listen up." The team gathered around her, and Beck pointed at the map. "Here's where we are. Here's where Black Moon Mine Road meets Highway 49. There's some kind of access road a half mile past that. We can take it to here, then follow the river, cross this gorge, and come at the mine from above, here. This also looks like a good place to park the comm gear and scopes. Any questions?"

The team exchanged glances, and all shook their heads.

"Good." Beck snapped the laptop shut. "Then I suggest we gear up and move out." She looked at Velasquez. "We'll take the Range Rover. The Jeep's too open and the Mini's too small Carver, so don't even think about it."

Carver paused mid-protest and shrugged. "Fair enough."

The team scooped up weapons, kit, scopes and headed out to trade bullets with the devil.

29

Even in the Range Rover, space was tight. Velasquez drove with Beck in the passenger seat. Carver and Gabriel sat in the back, watching the scenery go by. "Are we nearly there yet?"

"Quit it, Carver." Velasquez gunned the big truck past some Olde-Timey buildings along Main Street, avoiding the lemming-like tourists who tended to wander off the sidewalks and into the dirt road at random intervals. "Son of a—MOVE,

ASSHOLE." Velasquez hit the horn and a check-shorts-wearing Chad nearly jumped out of his skin as the big car swooped past.

"Maybe try not mowing down the civies, huh?" Beck gave Velasquez a little smile.

"Sorry."

The Range Rover reached the turnoff and swung onto Highway 49, picking up speed on the smooth surface. They started climbing into the mountains. Not a single other vehicle passed them.

"Kinda quiet, isn't it?" Carver frowned.

"Too quiet." Beck scowled at the empty road. The 49 was usually a busy road with plenty of tourist traffic heading both to Barlote and beyond. But today? Nothing. Beck's scowl intensified and she muttered quietly. "They're waiting for us. I can feel it."

Eventually, they reached the turn off. "Keep going." Beck's voice was sharp.

"What?" Velasquez flipped off the turn signal and kept going straight.

"Just because they've sent us an invitation doesn't mean we have to knock on the front door, right? I told you back at the hotel. Head up about a half mile. There's a second track that leads to the head frame."

Velasquez nodded. "Copy that."

A few seconds later, the access road appeared on the right. Velasquez pulled the Range Rover over and stopped. "Gate's locked."

Carver reached forward between the two chairs, a set of bolt-cutters in his hand. "Go ring the bell."

Velasquez looked at Beck, who gave her a nod. Velasquez grabbed the bolt cutters and grinned. "Back in a bit. Beck, bring the car through and I'll shut up shop behind us." She started to open the driver door, but Carver grabbed her shoulder.

"Hold."

Velasquez froze. "Problem?"

"Truck. Two o'clock."

The team sat motionless in the car until the truck had trundled past and around a bend.

Carver tapped Velasquez. "Okay. Clear."

Velasquez hopped out of the car and trotted over to the gate. Snipping through a link in the middle of the chain, she pushed the gate open, turned, and waved to Beck, who fired up the Range Rover and drove through.

As soon as the truck was clear of the gate, Velasquez pulled out a small, slightly tarnished carabiner from her pocket, pulled the gate closed and repositioned the chain. The carabiner sat in between two links, making the chain look like it was untouched. Velasquez picked up a branch and walking backwards towards the car, swept the tire tracks into oblivion. By the time she'd reached the Range Rover, anyone showing a passing interest at the gated track from the road would see nothing—it looked like nobody had been down there in years. Velasquez tossed the branch away into the scrub and hopped into the Range Rover as Beck scooted to the passenger seat. "Lock and load, my dudes. Let's go." She gave Beck a grin, handed Carver the bolt-cutters, and gunned the truck.

30

The access road went on for a winding quarter mile and stopped on a ridge above the old mine workings. The Range Rover was out of sight, but to be on the safe side, Velasquez nestled the big truck in among a copse of small trees. The foliage would disrupt the outline of the truck, making it practically invisible to a casual glance.

The team got out, taking care not to slam any doors. No point letting anyone know they had arrived this early in the operation. Carver opened the back and dropped the tailgate, exposing the checker plated sliding compartment loaded with ordnance.

"When this is over? We need to talk." Carver smiled at Velasquez, who gave him a wide-eyed, innocent look.

"What?" She shrugged and grinned. "A girl's gotta have some toys to play with, right?"

"Well, yes, but an M18?" Carver gingerly held up a Claymore land mine, the "FRONT TOWARD ENEMY" words nearly flaked off.

"I got that in a garage sale." Velasquez grinned. "I shit you not."

Carver shook his head, carefully replaced the M18, and started distributing kit to the team. The heavy ordnance they left behind. This was going to be a recon mission, so they needed to travel light. Backpacks for Beck and Velasquez, who also took the daylight scope and her pet sniper rifle. Just in case. After all, a girl's gotta have some toys. Carver loaded up on side-arms, ammo, and an M4.

Gabriel reached across him and picked up a simple duffel bag. "I think this is mine?"

Carver nodded. "All the tools of the trade, huh? Bell, book and candle?"

"Something like that." Gabriel hoisted the duffel bag across his shoulder. "We good?"

"We're good." Carver shut the back quietly and Velasquez hit the central locking. She'd disconnected the alarm so the usual "BEEPBEEP." was silenced this time.

Beck smiled at Velasquez. The girl may seem almost suicidally happy all the time, but she was a stickler for details.

Velasquez held up a finger. "Better set at least one alarm,

though, huh?" She unlocked the truck and opened the back one more time and scrabbled around in the compartment before shutting it again and locking up. She held up a grenade and grinned. "Surprise, motherfuckers." She positioned the grenade behind one of the truck's back wheels, carefully removed the pin, and made sure that the spring was pushed hard against the tire. If the truck moved even an inch, the spring would engage, and the grenade would detonate.

She straightened up, dusted her hands on her jeans and grinned. "Right. Now everyone, remember where we parked. And for fuck's sake, remember that the alarm is active, okay?" She rabbit-eared the word alarm and then jabbed a thumb at the grenade. "I don't wanna be making a hasty retreat and get my ass blown off by my own grenade. That would not be a good way to end a day's hike in the woods."

"Okay. Let's go." Beck led the way down a trail through the trees.

They went single file, carefully walking in each other's footsteps to disguise how many there were in the party. It was an old patrol trick, but it had worked for them on many occasions. After a few hundred yards, she stopped, reached into her rucksack, and pulled out a brown plastic tube with a metal tip.

"Trail-markers?" Gabriel watched her.

"Yep." Beck squeezed the plastic until a loud crack indicated something inside had broken. She shook the tube vigorously, then pushed it into the ground close to a tree trunk. "Thermal." She straightened up. "Stays hot enough to scope for up to twelve hours."

"Nifty." Velasquez grinned.

"Better than breadcrumbs." Beck grinned. "Let's keep moving."

The team followed the trail until it widened into a plateau with a very clearly defined edge. The air was filled with the distant boom of water. Further on, they came to the source of the sound—a raging white-water river, churning and boiling its way over massive boulders and gouging away at a thin strip of bank on the other side. The north bank butted up against a rock slope that looked slick with moss and algae. After around forty feet of slope stood a sheer granite cliff, covered in viciously sharp blades of stone that would slice a man in half in a heartbeat.

"Don't tell me." Carver sighed.

"Yep." Beck pointed to a ridge at the top of the hundred- and fifty-foot-high cliff. "That's our way in."

"That is not a way into anywhere. Besides, I haven't been on a rope since boot camp." Carver frowned. "Bulk's a bitch when you're fighting gravity. And I ain't exactly lightweight."

"Stop bellyaching, you pussy. You'll be fine." Beck crouched and rammed another trail-marker into the ground. She stood and examined the challenge ahead.

"I hate to be a moany-Minnie, but Carver's right. You might be a mountain goat, but the rest of us barely scraped through vertical ascents." Velasquez frowned. "You sure there's no other way around? Trying to get back across the river in the dark with kit is gonna be seriously hazardous to our health."

"It's the narrowest point for at least two hundred yards in any direction. It's hidden from view, and unless Beelzebub's got himself some high-tech drones, they won't see us coming."

"Okay, so while you may have the balance of a fucking mountain goat, we don't. This river's a bitch, and I'm not the world's greatest swimmer, either. Why don't we rig up a slider?" Carver scanned the opposite ridge and then looked to his left.

"We've got this tree as an anchor point this side. All we need are anchor points on the opposite side."

"Such as?" Beck scanned the treacherous cliff face and ridge. There were no trees on the opposite side close enough to serve as a second anchor point.

Carver held up a pair of pitons and grinned. "Mehhh, little mountain goatie."

"Shit." Beck sighed and snatched the pitons out of Carver's hand. "I hate you. You know that, right?"

"Off you trit-trot, little goatie. And watch out for any trolls hiding under those boulders." Carver grinned again.

"Fuck off." Beck shoved the pitons into her pocket, grabbed a length of rope and a belt full of carabiners, then faced the obstacle course ahead of her. A series of massive boulders, polished like glass and soaking wet, were surrounded by whirlpools and churning water that would quickly pull the unwary to a watery grave.

She gave the team a last look. "See you on the other side." She took a few steps back, eyed her first target, and launched herself at the river, disappearing into the mist.

It didn't take Beck long to reach the top of the north bank. Carver's goat-based taunts were spot on—Beck didn't miss her footing once. She landed on the north bank and gave Carver a thumbs up. "Securing." Her voice floated across the river.

On the opposite side, Carver hammered a piton into a fissure. He pulled one end of a rope through it and knotted it securely. He waved at Beck, who hauled on the rope, pulling it tight. She ran the rope to a nearby tree and looped the end around it, knotting it in position.

Carver picked up the other end of a second rope and threaded it through a second piton he'd mounted three feet from the first, giving them two tight ropes parallel to one another, about five feet from the surface of the water.

"Right then, Velasquez. Show us how it's done." Carver nodded toward the river.

Velasquez looped her arms across the ropes, using them for balance as she hopped and skipped across the boulders. She landed next to Beck and grinned. "Easy peasy."

Beck called out. "You're up."

Gabriel's crossing wasn't as spritely as Velasquez's and Beck's, resulting in a wet foot and some very un-monk-like swearing halfway across. He scrambled onto the north bank and glared back at the river as if it had personally insulted him.

Velasquez grinned. "Surprised you didn't walk across the water, monk."

"That's some pretty serious blasphemy right there."

"Sorry. Trying to have fun." Velasquez waved at Carver. "You joining us, big guy?"

Carver sighed, flung his arms across the ropes, and made his way over the river.

"That was the easy bit." Beck looked up at the granite cliff-face in front of them. "Now comes the hard bit." She looked at the team. "Okay. One last time. This is the point of no return. This is the recon. The mission's gonna be a whole lot uglier."

Carver, Velasquez, and Gabriel all looked at her. Velasquez, the usual grin fading from her lips, spoke quietly. "All for one, and all that shit. This is personal for me now. Those sons of bitches possessed me and Carver. We owe the motherfuckers some payback."

Beck nodded. "For sure."

Gabriel smiled. "Now, little mountain goat. You gonna lead us up this unscalable cliff face or what?"

Beck looked at the massive stone wall and at the forty-degree slope leading up its bottom. "First bit's pretty simple. Watch out for moss because that fucker's gonna be slippery. Let's go." Together, the team tackled the first section, scrambling over the surface and avoiding anything that looked too green or slimy.

Balancing at the top of the slope, they finally stood at the base of the granite cliff. Beck stood, hands on hips, staring up at the face, planning her route. "Okay." She sniffed and rubbed her nose, then turned to Carver. "Pack."

Carver unzipped the rucksack and held it open. Beck shoved a hand inside and pulled out a kit belt loaded with walnuts, cams, and carabiners—everything a climber would need to make a tricky ascent. She hooked the belt around her waist, attached a finger reel and put on a pair of climbing gloves. "I'll set the route and then send down a line. Tie up the webbing and rope and I'll haul it up. There's a set of belay devices in the pack, you know what to do. Carver, you follow, then Velasquez, then Gabe. If I stop, you stop. If I say go, you go. You take your mark from me, and you don't kick off any loose rocks on anyone below, got it?"

"You're crazy, you know that?" Carver shook his head.

"You say that every time we climb. Yet here we all are, right?"

"Right."

"Good. So shut your mouth and kit up. I'm gonna go climbing."

Beck walked along the base of the wall, scanning for the easiest route. For her, this was a walk in the park. But she knew that both Carver and Velasquez were not good climbers, and Gabriel hadn't climbed in years. Fifteen yards away, she found a crevasse that went at least half-way up the wall. Where it ended, a second crack started that ran all the way up to the top. She couldn't judge the gap between the crevice and the crack, but it was do-able, she was certain. Beck smiled. Ask and the gods shall deliver.

Beck grabbed a lip of rock, put her boot on another ledge, and lifted herself onto the cliff-face. Those first moves were always the most nerve-wracking, but once she was above ground, Beck was in her happy place. She'd climbed in Moab. She'd climbed Indian Creek. Hell, she'd even climbed Yosemite's El Capitan, regarded as the toughest climbing challenge in the world. The feeling of absolute freedom, with every move putting you seconds away from death—there was nothing quite like it.

She felt focused, calm, confident. For the first time in weeks. She felt like herself again.

Hand over hand, she climbed. Forgetting about the end of the world. Forgetting about Lightbringers. She even forgot about Cathy for a few minutes.

There was nothing except her and the climb.

Fifteen feet up, she inserted a walnut into a crack and pulled herself onto the next ledge. She set the line, checked it, and then looked up. A little smile flickered across her face. A slight overhang. Only a few degrees, but enough to turn a relatively easy climb into more of a test of skill. Her fingers reached up, probing for a hold, and she pulled herself upwards.

After a series of stops to insert more walnuts and to set a line that even Carver could follow, Beck reached the end of the crevice. She was seventy-five feet up. She set a walnut, hooked up, and glanced down. Gabriel, Carver and Velasquez were still at the foot of the cliff, waiting for her to reach the top. She nodded and then glanced up at the crack.

"Shit."

Beck gritted her teeth. The crack was farther than she'd anticipated. She was going to have to do a Hail Mary on this one. She called down to Carver. "Get ready to catch me."

"What? Are you shitting me, woman?" Carver froze, staring up. If Beck fell from that height, there was no way anyone was catching her. "I hate when she does this. It's Utah all over again. Shit."

Beck brought her boot tip up to a tiny ledge and balanced like a demented spider with her knee almost touching her waist. She inched her fingers towards the crack but couldn't reach it. Beck readjusted her position, pulling back with her left hand and adjusting her boot to an even higher ledge. She grabbed a cam from her belt, hooked a carabiner into the loop, and tried again, every muscle straining and burning.

Squeezing the cam gears, she pushed the head into the crack. As the cam locked home, her boot slipped. With a yelp, she slid across the cliff wall and pitched forward. Her left hand yanked free and for a few heart-stopping seconds she hung, facing outward, on her right hand. She closed her eyes, praying that the cam would hold.

It did.

She opened her eyes, took a couple of slow breaths to bring her heartrate down, and flipped around to face the cliff wall again. Carefully, purposefully, she let her climbing instincts kick in, and after a couple of attempts, her right boot found a ledge. Beck rested for a moment, letting her left boot hang in the air. Then with a grunt, she reached up and started climbing again.

Below her, the team let out a collective sigh of relief.

The last section went smoothly, and a few minutes later Beck's hand reached over the top, scrabbling for something to grab. Roots, a tuft of grass, anything. Eventually, her fingers found some exposed roots and she hauled herself onto the top of the cliff. She scrambled to her feet and trotted along the ledge until she came to a stout pair of trees about ten feet back from the edge. She unhooked the finger reel from her belt and sent the clip down, unspooling the yellow nylon string.

Velasquez watched the clip bounce its way down the cliff. She caught the clip and hooked a bundle of webbing and rope to it. Once everything was secured, she gave the string two sharp tugs, and watched the bundle inch up the cliff as Beck reeled it in.

After she'd dragged the webbing and rope up the cliff, Beck unclipped the bundle, flung the webbing around the tree trunk and attached the rope to the webbing. She scooped up the bundle in her arms and carried it to the edge of the cliff. "HEADS UP." She dumped the bundle over the edge.

Below her, the team stepped back as the rope swooshed down the cliff and hit the ground. Carver attached a pair of belay devices to the rope while Velasquez secured the bottom to a piton she'd rammed into the base of the wall.

Carver gave the rope two tugs to let Beck know they were ready and turned to Gabriel. "Women and monks first, my man."

Gabriel sighed, reached into his shirt, and pulled out a crucifix. He kissed it and made the sign of the cross with his right hand.

"C'mon, man. Tú puedes hacerlo." Velasquez aimed a boot at Gabriel's ass.

"Okay. Okay. I'm going." Gabriel dodged the boot and started climbing, sliding each belay device up the rope a few feet before locking it in place and taking another step.

Carver and Velasquez watched him make his way up the cliff. Without looking away, Velasquez punched Carver on the arm.

"Ow. Quit it. What was that for?"

"The women and monks first bullshit, you asshole."

Carver chuckled.

Above them, Gabriel continued up the cliff to the ledge. As his head popped over the edge, he saw a hand in front of his face. He followed the hand up to Beck's grinning face. "Just like riding a bicycle, isn't it?" She gripped his extended hand and with surprising strength, pulled him onto the top. He rolled away and sat up, legs dangling over the edge. Gabriel unclipped from the line and Beck sent the belay devices back down the rope into Velasquez's waiting hands. She kept her eyes on the woman until Velasquez scrambled over the top a few moments later.

"What a rush." Velasquez unhooked from the belay devices and Beck sent them back down one last time. Before Carver hitched up, she gave the webbing one last check, making sure it hadn't shifted position. She leaned over the edge and called down.

"You're good to go, big guy."

"Not so much of the big." Carver stared up at the cliff face and muttered. "I hate heights. Hate 'em. Hate 'em."

31

T he sun turned blood red, sending fingers of purple and orange across the sky, wrapping the distant Sierra Nevada mountains in a kaleidoscope of colors. The team stood on the edge of the cliff, facing west. Directly below them, one hundred yards away down a shallow slope, sprawled the twenty-five-acre mining compound. Although much of it looked abandoned, the chain-link fence and razor wire coils seemed remarkably new.

"Jackpot." Beck spoke quietly. She pulled the tripod out of the kit bag and set it up. "Perfect for you and the comms gear, Velasquez." She mounted the scope onto the tripod.

"Good angle. Clear range of shots if necessary. Me likey." Velasquez's usual grin was absent. She was in business mode.

"First thing we need to figure out is which building they're sleeping in." Beck put her eye to the scope and started scanning the compound.

"Do you reckon they're getting any sleep at all? What with the whole 'end of the world,' Armageddon thing going on?" Carver frowned and pulled a pair of binoculars from his pack.

"They're getting their beauty sleep, you can count on it. This group likes its lambs compliant and well rested." Beck continued to examine every aspect of the compound. "At the other place, it was like a dormitory. Adults separate from children. Men separate from women." She straightened. "Makes it easier, as long as we can narrow down our target area." She looked again through the scope. The 140-foot head frame dominated the middle of the grounds, surrounded by a selection of buildings in various states of disrepair. Some were partially collapsed while others appeared to have been completely restored.

"I'm guessing the ones we need to focus our efforts on are the ones with the shiny white paint," Carver said.

Beck leaned away from the scope and faced him. "Not necessarily. Remember, we're not dealing with Waco whackos here. These bastards are organized, clever, and devious as fuck."

She returned her eye to the scope and focused on the white bus parked on a hill near the front gate. Next to the bus stood a three-story building with a wraparound covered porch and second-floor balcony. Beck straightened again. "Bingo." She motioned to the building. "Carver. There. By the bus. That's ground zero. The other buildings are a distraction."

Carver focused on the building. "If the sleeping arrangements are the same, all the men will be on the first floor. That'll make ingress tricky."

"But not impossible." Velasquez tapped Carver's shoulder, who moved to let her look.

"True." Beck nodded. "If the kids are on the third floor, we can climb up the back corner. Take Cathy right out of the front window."

"Okay, but what about a way in?" Velasquez gave up the scope to Beck.

Beck moved the scope in the opposite direction towards a pair of ATVs parked in front of a narrow building six feet away from the fence. "Blindspot. There. The building gives us all the cover we need. We could take out a whole section without them even knowing we were there."

"Ooo. I spy, with my little eye, something beginning with kaboom." Carver grinned and passed his binoculars to Velasquez, who smiled broadly.

"Two fifty-five-gallon drums. Fuel dump. Shit, they've even left the nozzle in one of them." She chuckled. "I can put a C4 brick on that and blow it to shit if we need a distraction. Should be bang enough to cover us getting the hell out of Dodge and back up here."

"I concur." Beck focused on the barrels.

"Incoming." Gabriel pointed towards a cloud of dust moving along the main track. A white truck bounced its way over ruts and potholes before rolling to a stop outside the main gate. A horn honked and a sentry appeared, an AR-15 slung over one shoulder. He peered at the van, nodded, and unlocked the gate.

"At least we know their firepower now." Carver watched the guard carefully.

The truck moved through the gate and the sentry locked up behind it before returning to the gatehouse. The truck stopped in a cloud of dust outside the main building. The door opened, and a curly-haired, bearded man got out.

Beck let out a gasp. "Shit. It's Pete."

"Pete as in ex Pete?" Carver swung his binoculars towards the man.

"How many other 'shit it's Pete' Petes do you think I'd be referring to? Of course it's my ex, the poisonous little shit." Beck stared through the scope and watched Pete open the van. A woman in the Lightbringer uniform of polo shirt and slacks got out, guiding another figure carefully out of the van. The other figure had his hands tied behind his back and a bag over his head.

"Fuck. They got Kip. And that's Bobbi with him."

"What?" Gabriel pushed Beck away and stared through the scope. "Damn it. DAMN IT." He reeled away and kicked at a stone.

Beck took another look through the scope as Bobbi and a second gun-toting sentry led the bagged and tagged Kip into the building. She frowned. "That complicates things."

"Not really. He doesn't know enough to give us away. But we can't leave him there." Gabriel looked deeply troubled.

"We have to."

"Here we go again. No, we don't have to leave him." Gabriel glared at Beck.

"We can't save everyone."

"That seems to be your default setting." He mimicked her. "We can't save everyone."

Beck glared at Gabriel. "You wanna do this now? Seriously?"

Gabriel ignored her, his eyes darkening. "You first came out with that peach back in Al-Qa'im, remember? And you were wrong then too. We did save everyone. You gotta try a bit harder and remember this is bigger than Cathy. We're talking end of the world scenario here. And that means we do our darndest to save as many souls as we can. Including Kip." He stood. "Are we done here?"

Beck sighed and folded the scope up. "We're done. We have all the intel we need. Let's get back."

The team packed quietly and moved away from the ridge as the sun started to sink.

Below them, Pete frowned, and glanced up at the ridge. His blue eyes swirled and turned black. He stared intently at the spot where the team had been seconds earlier.

32

The hike to the truck had been uneventful, if a little on the "off the beaten track" side. No random guards had discovered their trail, or if they had, they hadn't done anything about it. Velasquez carefully removed the booby-trapped grenade from the wheel, and they made their way to the gate, Velasquez again sweeping any trace of the tire tracks so that no cursory glances would reveal that anyone had been down the track recently. She left the carabiner in place, for when they returned later.

The team drove back in silence. There was a palpable tension between Beck and Gabriel. Velasquez focused on the drive, while Carver sat in the back, staring out the window, trying to make his bulk as small as possible. It was like being in the same room with a couple who'd had the biggest Thanksgiving fight of all time. But with more guns.

They reached the hotel at dusk, and the team split up into their respective rooms.

Gabriel sat on his bed, staring at the cracked and peeling floorboards as Carver clambered out of his OCP fatigues and into night camo. Carver hopped on one leg as he struggled into the pants and glanced over at Gabriel. "You okay?"

"I dunno. What did she say when I came upstairs?"

"The usual list of shit."

"No surprise there, then."

Carver sat down heavily on the bed and glared at the camo pant leg that had wrapped itself around his foot and refused to budge. He grabbed the leg and shook it like a dog with a rag until it finally unwound itself and slid over his heel and into position. "Finally. I swear my wife put these on a hot wash and they've shrunk."

"You're married?"

Carver grinned. "Yep. And compared to Beck and her reliable level of barely suppressed rage at the world and all its contents, my wife's a fucking weathervane in a tornado. Think yourself lucky with Beck. At least you know what state of mind she's going to be in at any one time." He ticked them off on his fingers. "Pissed, really pissed, fucking furious, and oh lordy, she's a-comin'." Carver shrugged and grinned. "Don't worry, I'm

African-American. I can use that one ironically and you don't need to be offended on my behalf." He laughed. "Anyway, right now, I'd say she's barely at 'really pissed.' So you're fine for the moment."

Gabriel gave Carver a little smile. "I'm still unpacking that you're married, dude."

"Two kids as well. And no, I'm not showing you their picture. We know how that ends in the movies, right? The guy shows his buddies a picture of his gal right before the big oppo and gets a bullet between the eyes the second he gets out of the helo. Fuck that." Carver laughed.

"I'm pleased you've found someone, man." Gabriel sighed.

"You still beating yourself up over Velasquez?" Carver frowned.

"That's all water under the bridge. We worked things out a long time ago. Besides, I think she's happier now, you know?"

Carver nodded. "I know. They make a good couple." He stood up and wandered over to the window. Pulling the net back a fraction, he spotted two preppy-dressed young men in polo shirts and chinos. "We're being watched."

"Of course we are. Nobody said the Lightbringers were stupid." Gabriel stood and joined his friend. "I'm surprised there's only two of them."

Carver shrugged and let the net drop back into place. "You gonna wear that monk's robe forever now?"

Gabriel stared out the window and thought for a moment. "Two days ago, I would've said yes without a moment's hesitation."

"And now?"

"I guess everyone who takes holy orders has those dark moments of self-doubt."

"So you're self-doubting? Is it something we said?" Carver's friendly grin dissolved, and he looked serious for a moment. "Because if we've done anything to shake your faith, I promise you, it wasn't done deliberately."

Gabriel laid a hand on Carver's shoulder and smiled gently. "Faith is a complex thing. It's a long, long path that can sometimes get a little confusing and sends you in a direction you weren't expecting. Like now."

"I hear you. We're all stumbling around in the dark, stubbing our toes on what ifs and maybes. Wishing we could hit the rewind button and get a do-over. Only we can't."

"Is that supposed to make me feel better?" Gabriel chuckled. "Because it ain't."

Carver shook his head. "No, my brother. It's not. All I'm saying is... shit man, look, go easy on yourself, okay? And go easy on those around you, too."

"Like Beck?"

Carver nodded. "Yeah. Like Beck. And everyone else, too. We're all fighting our own demons, as well as those sons of bitches in that compound. Just because you can't see our demons doesn't make them any less scary to us, you know?"

"I'm sorry. I've been a bit of an asshole, haven't I?"

Carver laughed. "You always were. Only now you're a sanctimonious asshole with a monk's habit, but we still love you, brother. Always have, always will." He clapped Gabriel on the shoulder. "Lights out, my man. We need to get some sleep, okay?" He strolled over to the switch and flicked it off, plunging the room into darkness. He shuffled across the room towards his bed, swearing briefly as his toe met the corner of the bed post.

"Just stumbling around in the dark, stubbing your toe on a what if?"

"Fuck you." Carver laughed, rolled into bed, and was asleep in seconds.

Gabriel lay in the dark, listening to the gentle snores of his friend, and wondering where his path would take him next.

33

The sky was ablaze with stars. On the outcrop above the compound, Velasquez peered through a scope and grinned. "My, my, aren't they busy little bees this evening." She pulled away from the scope. "Oh, eww. What is it with guys and marking their territory, seriously? The latrines are right there, you dirty bird."

Beck chuckled. "You never heard of the phrase, 'pissing contest' then?"

"Honey, you were around the Brits way more than me out in Afghan. Their weird-assed phrases rubbed off on you more than they did me." She went to the scope. "But in this case, that about sums it up. I shit you not, Lightbringer number two has only come along and pissed in the exact same spot."

"So other than a bunch of tomcats peeing everywhere, anything else in the scope?"

"One in the gatehouse. That's it."

"Keep looking."

Velasquez nodded and scanned the compound. Black Moon Mine was living up to its name—despite the effervescent Milky Way above their heads, the darkness was as thick as molasses. The floodlights lighting the main quadrant did nothing to push back the shadows that clustered around the fence, gate, and buildings. There were a million and one spots to hide in this oh-so-secure whacko-Waco-wannabe enclosure. Velasquez focused on a tall structure in the middle of the square. "That's the mine shaft under the tall thing in the middle, right?"

Beck nodded. "Yep."

"Lots and lots of heat coming out of there, honey."

A rustling in the bushes made both Beck and Velasquez draw their sidearms and focus two Glock's worth of female aggression at a small rabbitbrush bush. The bush sprouted two arms, raised skyward. "Don't shoot." Gabriel emerged, hands still up.

"Then don't creep up like that, dumbass." Beck put the gun back in its holster. "All okay with the truck?"

"All good." Gabriel crouched next to Beck. "What we got?"

"A ton of heat coming outta the mine shaft." Velasquez got to the scope and focused in on the mine opening. "Probably a generator or something."

Beck and Gabriel traded looks. "Yeah. Or something." Beck studied the compound.

"Wait, we've got movement." Velasquez scanned the compound. "Okay. A heat signature rabbited out of the building next to the ATVs. Heading across the compound. Looks like he's going into where they took Kip earlier." She leaned back. "We're on."

Beck stood up, letting the blood recirculate back into her legs—she'd been crouched in the same position for too long and the sharp tingling in her feet felt like a thousand needles stabbing into her skin at once. She ignored the sensation and studied the compound. "Okay. we'll take care of the guard first."

"Comms check, people." Gabriel adjusted his headset and tapped his throat mic. "Velasquez?"

"Estoy aquí, cariño."

Gabriel smiled fleetingly at Velasquez and then spoke again. "Carver?"

"Check."

"Beck?"

"Fuck you and the horse you rode in on."

"Such anger, but I'll take it." Gabriel gave Beck a thumbs up. "Comms are good to go."

"Right. Let's move." Beck, Carver, and Velasquez took up position. "Eyes on, monk. We're relying on you to call it, okay?"

"I've got your back. Good luck."

Beck turned and looked at Gabriel, waiting for a smart-ass comment that never came. "You really mean that, don't you?"

"You know I do. Go with God." Gabriel gave her a soft smile.

Beck stared at him for a second, nodded curtly, and set off towards the compound.

Gabriel watched his three friends vanish into the darkness, and crossed himself, mouthing a silent prayer.

34

Beck, Carver and Velasquez approached the chain-link fence in a dead spot between the watch towers. Beck scanned the compound for movement, and then spoke softly into her comms. "How we looking?"

"All clear." Gabriel's voice was soft but crystal-clear over the military-grade comms. There was no hissing or crackling. It was almost like he was next to them, rather than nearly a quarter of a mile away.

"Copy that." Beck silently waved Velasquez through.

Velasquez soundlessly crept to the fence and made quick work of the links with a set of bolt cutters, then pushed the fence aside like a curtain. "Hustle, people. We're exposed here." Velasquez whispered at Beck and Carver. They didn't need telling twice. The team moved silently forward, Velasquez repositioning the cut section as carefully as she could. The more things looked normal, the longer they would have before any kind of alarm was raised.

The team paused. Beck scanned ahead and then nodded. "Carver. You're up." Beck pointed at a 55-gallon drum with a fuel nozzle attached.

The big man tipped the drum onto one edge and rolled it around the side of the building, positioning it approximately ten feet from the cut in the fence. He let the drum down easy, getting it into place without making a sound. He unhooked a radio-controlled explosive "spark." The device was no bigger than a cigarette packet. He carefully pressed the spark onto the side of the drum and armed it. A dim red LED flashed on the device. Carver reached into his pocket and pulled out a roll of electrical tape. He tore a piece off and positioned it over the LED. It might've been small, but in the darkness the light stood out like a beacon.

Carver checked the connection with the remote trigger and nodded at Beck.

Beck tapped her throat mic. "Gabe, still clear?"

"Affirmative."

"Okay. Let's move."

The team headed towards the building on the left. They knew they had at least one sentry to deal with inside. The trick was going to be neutralizing him without alerting any of the others. Velasquez positioned herself under a window, and carefully raised her head above the sill.

The inside of the building was dimly lit, but it was obviously the visitor center when it wasn't operating as the main reception area for an end-of-the-world cult. The high vaulted ceiling was lost in shadows, and the only illumination was a low-powered desk lamp. It gave the lines of books, gifts, and displays of mining equipment an eerie, ghostly look. The only other source of illumination was an open door at the end, where bright light spilled out in a fan shape across the floor. Next to the door sat the sentry, engrossed in a Bible. On his right sat a bank of black and white monitors, each screen showing a different part of the compound. The grainy pictures were hard to distinguish, but Velasquez could see that if they didn't move now, camera three would soon give them away. "Shit." She ducked down and frantically motioned to Beck and Carver to follow her around the building to a dead spot not covered by the cameras.

The three figures crouch-scuttled around the corner, pressing themselves as closely as possible to the dark shadows until they were sure they were out of view.

Inside the building, the sentry's radio crackled. "Hey, Matt?"

The Bible-reading sentry sighed and put down his book. He scooped up the radio and pressed talk. "What's up, Hank?"

"I'm not sure, but I think I saw movement in the yard by you. Wanna check it out?"

"Something? As in, what? A racoon? A person? What?"

"Dude, I know what a racoon looks like. This looked like people."

"People plural? You sure?"

"If I was sure I'd be hitting the alarm. But if I'm wrong,

Pastor Reid won't exactly be pleased, will he? Check it out. Keep your radio on."

"Right." The sentry stood up, checked the bank of CCTV monitors, and picked up a flashlight and a sidearm from the table. He clicked on the flashlight, which flickered briefly. A quick double-slap settled the beam, and he headed for the door.

At the back of the building, three crouched figures huddled in the shadows. Beck whispered into her mic. "Talk to me, Gabe."

Up on the ridge, Gabriel scanned the compound. The heat sensor in the scope picked up a signature in the room on top of the headframe. "Damn it. We missed one. Top of the tower. He looks real interested in the building you're next to. Hold your position."

The visitor center door opened, spilling a dim wash of light into the quadrant. The sharp-edged beam of the sentry's flashlight blasted across the dirt.

"Shit. Shit. Beck, you've got company."

"Directions."

"Inside."

"Say again?"

"Get inside. Now."

"You have got to be fucking kidding." Beck faced the others and indicated the door. "In. Now."

The team hopped in through the door as the sentry rounded the corner of the building. He swung his flashlight to the spot where Velasquez, Beck and Carver had been hiding seconds before. He rolled his eyes and pressed the talk button on his radio. "Hey Hank? You really need to get your eyes checked buddy. Nothing here except tumbleweeds."

"I could've sworn I saw movement."

"Nothing. I'm going back inside." The sentry clicked off his flashlight and headed to the front of the visitor center. He strolled inside and shut the door, muttering quietly. "Asshole." He wandered over to the chair, gave the CCTV monitors a quick glance, and sat. As he picked up his Bible, a slender arm snaked around his neck into a chokehold.

Velasquez squeezed, locking her hand against her bicep, and dropping her elbow to get the sleeper hold right. "Nighty night, don't let the bed-bugs bite."

The sentry struggled briefly, clawing at Velasquez's arm, desperate to break her grip. He reached a shaking hand towards his radio, only to watch Carver emerge from the shadows, pick up the radio and put it out of reach. Carver wagged a finger at the sentry, who finally succumbed to Velasquez's sleeper hold. His eyes rolled back, and he slumped.

Velasquez released her grip and gently lowered the guard to the ground. She pulled a zip-tie out and secured the guard's hands behind his back. A few wraps of tape secured his ankles together. "He'll be out for a while, but we shouldn't wait around too long." She pointed at the unconscious guard. "Carver? Do you mind bringing Mister Sleepy along with us? I'd rather he was locked in a cupboard or something and not on show for any stray Lightbringer to find."

"Good call." Carver bent and hoisted the man onto his shoulders. "Righty then. Any unconscious guy-sized boxes around here?"

Beck pointed to a door. "Model room. It's windowless, dark, and there's plenty of places to hide dozy there. Let's go." She headed towards the door and turned the handle.

The model room was pitch black. Beck clicked the switch next to the door frame and ancient, yellowing fluorescent tube lights clinked, hummed, and flickered into life. One steadfastly resisted to stay lit for a few seconds before finally blinking out completely. It left a suitably dark corner behind a large case where the unconscious sentry could be left without anyone seeing him. Carver unceremoniously dumped the man on the floor, kicking his feet out of the line of sight from the door. "As long as he stays out, we should be okay for a while."

Velasquez grinned. "Trust me, he'll stay out." She looked towards a glass cabinet. "Wow. Is this for real?"

Beck nodded. "Yep. Three hundred miles of tunnels. One of the biggest mine complexes in north America."

"And a real pain in the ass for us." Carver joined Velasquez and Beck at the case and stared at the three-dimensional model. "Pretty cool to look at, though."

"You guys okay down there?" Gabriel's voice cracked over the comms.

"All good. Looking at a model of the underground complex. It's vast."

"We knew that. Any sign of Kip?"

Beck frowned. "In the model room?"

"C'mon, Beck. We talked about this."

Velasquez unhooked her sidearm and screwed a suppressor to the barrel. "Won't take a minute to look for him. The guy could be in some heavy-shit level danger."

"We don't have time."

"We make time." Velasquez's normally happy-go-lucky voice was sharp. She checked the Glock and headed for the door.

Beck turned. "Wait."

"Beck..."

"We're coming with." Beck frowned. "And no, we can't go via the gift shop."

"I wasn't even gonna say that." Carver looked hurt.

"Let's go. Keep it quiet, keep it neat." Beck nodded to Velasquez, who led the way out of the model room and into the main hall.

A brisk survey of several doors yielded no clue as to Kip's location. A storage closet and a bathroom held no evidence of habitation. Then Carver opened a third door and froze.

"Shit. Shit, shit, shit." He backed up. Beck and Velasquez peered through the door.

"That's fucking sick, man." Velasquez turned away, the blood drained from her face.

"What's going on?" Gabriel's voice sounded concerned.

"These people just told me all I need to know about them." She stared at the scene in front of her. "Kip's dead. Very, very dead."

Beck walked slowly into the room, treading carefully, and listening for the slightest sound that would indicate some sick son of a bitch Lightbringer was in there with her. She almost hoped there would be so she could work out some of the boiling rage churning inside her.

At the far end of the room, surrounded by unlit pillar candles and scribbled chalk glyphs was a large wooden X frame. Attached to the frame, spread-eagled and upside down, was Kip. His lifeless eyes stared out and a wide gash across his throat still dripped the blood into a large plastic orange bucket underneath.

They'd been very professional.

Not a single drop of Kip's precious blood had been spilled.

Velasquez spoke quietly into the comms. "Él está muerto. Lo siento." She dropped her hand to her side. "He was an okay guy. He didn't deserve this shit."

"No. He didn't." Beck gave the bucket a hard kick, sending the blood spilling across the floor and splattering the walls. "Motherfuckers."

Up on the ridge, Gabriel, gripping the scope with his left hand, let his head drop and closed his eyes for a moment. He crossed himself and mouthed a silent prayer for Kip's soul.

Back in the room, Carver laid a hand on Beck's shoulders. "There's nothing we can do for him now. We need to keep going." He clicked the comms. "Gabe? Can you tell if that guy in the tower has eyes on us?"

There was a moment's pause, then Gabriel's voice came over the comms. "The tower's totally black. I don't see him. That could be good, or it could be real bad."

Carver frowned. "Okay. I'm moving. Keep a watch and guide me to the tower."

"Copy that. Go now."

Carver gave Beck a quick grin. "Stay lucky."

Beck grinned back. "Stay upright."

Carver nodded, crept to the door, and then made a run for the tower. At the tower base, he did a lap, looking for the ladder until he found it on the shadowy underside. He scrambled up as quickly as a cat. As he climbed, he spoke quietly. "Anything?"

"No visuals. Looks like you're clear."

Back in the visitor center, Beck watched Carver make the tower. "Damn. For a big guy, he moves fast, doesn't he?"

Velasquez peered over Beck's shoulder and smiled. "What was it that British SAS captain said about him in Kandahar?" she put on a mock British accent, "Like a bloody rat up a drainpipe with its ass on fire." Velasquez chuckled. "He's clear. We need to get moving."

"Arse."

"What?"

"The Brits say arse."

"Really?"

"Yep."

Velasquez chuckled again. "Man, they're weird. Shall we?"

They turned to go and froze as the sentry's radio squawked into life. "Hey Matt? It's Hank. You better check outside again bud. I swear I saw someone crossing the yard to the headframe, and I'm pretty sure it wasn't one of our people. Matt? You hear me?"

Velasquez looked at Beck. "Shit."

"Matt. Come in, Matt. Matt?" The radio squawked again. "Josh, get over to the visitor center. Matt isn't answering his radio."

Another deeper voice responded. "On my way."

Beck motioned to the door and Velasquez moved silently towards the exit.

On the ridge, Gabriel watched the figure of the gatehouse sentry moving across the yard. "Carver, you've got about five seconds. Distract him and then get the hell off that ladder and take the tower guard out."

Carver swore and hoarsely whispered into the comms. "I thought you said he was gone."

"My bad."

"My bad? You asshole." Carver pulled the signaling whistle from his jacket and hurled it towards the shack above. It clattered into the corner of the tower shack and the sentry whipped his head around, distracted by the noise.

Carver used the split second to vault into the tower shack, ready to take the sentry out.

The sentry was fast.

Way too fast for a normal minimum wage grunt of a guard. He spun around and hissed. His eyes glowed a bright orange.

"Oh, shit." Carver stared at the sentry watching for any micromovement that would tell him which way the guard was going to spring. The sentry leapt like a panther, hands outstretched like claws. Carver ducked and swung his rifle up but was a millisecond too slow. The sentry, hissing and clawing at him like a possum with rabies, knocked the rifle from Carver's hands, sending it skittering towards the ladder. The rifle stopped an inch from the edge.

"Oh, fuck this." Carver unsheathed a Ka-Bar and swung it in an upward arc. Again, the sentry dodged the blade in a blur. It almost seemed as if whatever possessed the man allowed him to move through time and space at a different speed from Carver. The big man saw a succession of guards like ghosts following the arc of the man's movement and then re-joining into a single form again an inch away from Carver's slashing blade. The man hissed again and barreled forward, slamming into Carver with incredible force. He was half Carver's size, yet hit him with the force of a bear. Carver hit the back wall of the shack with a "Whoof" as the air pushed hard out of his lungs.

Below the tower shack, Josh heard the thump and stopped, looking up. He raised the radio to his mouth. "Hank? You okay up there?"

In the shack, Carver responded. Hank may have had the element of surprise for the first attack, but Carver knew exactly what he was dealing with now. He rallied, pushed his heel against the wall, and returned the favor, with interest. The slight frame of Hank flew across the tower shack and crashed into the opposite wall, falling to the floor with a bang. Dust and splinters rained down from overhead, and the whole structure vibrated with the impact.

Josh scowled and spoke into his radio again. "Hank? What's going on up there?"

Hank, however, was a little busy. He'd gone completely feral and hissed like a kettle at Carver. He blasted towards the big man, grappling him into a bearhug and pushing him relentlessly towards the edge of the tower. He stared into Carver's eyes, black swirling orbs filled with hate. "Can you fly, big guy? Huh?" Hank's face split into a manic grin. "Can you?"

Carver had less than one second to reach out and grab the ladder. He pirouetted around the frame, his body slamming into the shack's outer wall. Hank, however, kept on going. Carver's sudden change in direction gave the Lightbringer far more momentum than he wanted, and he lost his grip on Carver.

Gravity took charge, and Carver watched Hank plummet to the ground. "Nope. And neither, it seems, can you."

Josh managed to dive out of the way as Hank landed. The noise was like a sock full of porridge and twigs getting slam-dunked into a brick floor. Bones snapped audibly, and the damp, squelching sound of Hank's internal organs turning into jelly was deeply unsettling. The sentry stared at Hank for a couple of seconds, then looked up at Carver, who was still hanging precariously by one hand from the ladder.

"You son of a bitch." Josh ditched the radio and swung up his AR-15. His finger almost made it to the trigger. He heard a sound in the distance like a branch breaking and his cheek exploded in a fountain of blood and bone.

The bullet ricocheted off his jaw and exited from his neck, obliterating a section of the carotid artery in the process. He dropped silently, clutching his throat in a vain attempt to stop the pulsing flow of blood that spurted across the dirt. Eventually, he stopped twitching and lay still, his blood-soaked hand flopping away from his throat.

Velasquez lowered her gun. "Hella shot."

"Two down. A shit-ton more to go." Beck spoke into the comms. "Any more hostiles?"

"Negative."

She nodded and glanced up. "You with us, big guy?"

Carver looked down from the tower and grinned. "Yes, ma'am."

"All right. Double-time it back down that ladder and let's get these two out of sight." She looked down at the bloodstain in the dirt. "Not much we can do to cover that up, but you can't have everything your way, I guess." She grabbed what was left of Hank and dragged him towards the visitor center.

Velasquez wrinkled her nose at the blood-caked Josh and sighed. "This jacket was new, for fuck's sake." She shrugged, grabbed Josh's feet, and started hauling him out of sight.

Carver dropped the last few feet to the ground and followed the two women, kicking the dust around to try and hide the drag marks. Hank and Josh's final resting place was behind a dumpster filled with trash from the visitor center.

Beck dusted her hands, and silently signaled to Carver and Velasquez. They set off at a run towards the mine offices, and the next stage of the operation.

35

Despite the kerfuffle, the alarm stayed resolutely unraised. Beck offered up a silent prayer to the god of ninjas, if there was one, and led the team to the side of the mine office building. A surprisingly large, gulag-like structure, the office block offered plenty of ingress points. This was both a good and a bad thing. Ingress meant easy access. But it also meant that if the ninja god abandoned them and all Hell broke loose, they'd have combatants coming at them from every direction.

It was a risk Beck was prepared to take.

The mine offices backed up against a hill, and at the side ran a steep set of concrete steps. Beck pulled out her night scope and scanned the ridgeline. She spoke quietly into the comms. "Gabe, anything?"

"Ridge is clear. No movement."

"Copy. Okay. Comms going dark until we're out or shit goes south. Any problems, give me three clicks."

"Understood."

She stowed the nightscope, turned to Velasquez and Carver. "Best sneaky feet on, kiddos." She pointed at an arbor that framed the entrance to the porch. "Carver, string that up with one of your Three Stooges specials and meet us upstairs, okay?"

"Will do." Carver moved silently towards the arbor, pulling out a reel of wire as he cat-walked over to the ivy-covered arch.

Beck and Velasquez left Carver to his task and moved up the stairs to the second-floor balcony. The two women melted into the shadows, moving silently and purposefully, the business end of their guns almost sniffing the air. Beck turned to Velasquez, who nodded a "clear" signal to her partner. Beck pointed towards the third-floor balcony. Velasquez affirmed, and the women made their way up the staircase to the next level.

Beck hopped onto the roof and scuttled along before dropping down onto the balcony. She carefully peeped into a window, cupping her hands to cut out any external light so she could see inside more clearly.

Sleeping peacefully in the moonlight lay six children, snuggled up in sleeping bags. Two rows of three cots were positioned on opposite walls, with a wide walkway down the middle.

Beck gave the window a try. The lower sash wouldn't budge. "Shit." Beck flipped down her night-vision goggles and focused on the latch. A small pocketknife appeared in her hands, and she slipped the thin blade under the latch, sliding it gently between the frame and the sill.

"What's your progress?"

Beck's hand slipped as she jumped at the sound of Gabriel's voice in her ear. The blade made a scraping noise as it contacted the metal catch. The child nearest the window mumbled and wriggled in her sleeping bag. Beck held her breath and waited for the child to become still again. She shifted away from the window and pressed her back against the wall. She glared at the ridge where she knew Gabriel was watching her through his scope and whispered hoarsely into the comms. "What bit of going dark didn't you get? Jesus. You frightened the life out of me."

"Sorry, but this is important."

"We got company?" Beck scanned the yard below. All seemed quiet.

"No. But before you go in, I want you to listen to me."

"Kinda fucking busy here." Beck scowled towards Gabriel's position. "This had better be damn important."

"It is. If Cathy has one of those things inside her then remember, that is what you're fighting, okay? Not Cathy. Don't let your feelings get in the way. Restrain her by any means necessary and get her to me as quickly as you can. Don't try any sappy, mother-daughter reunions at this point. You understand? Beck?"

Beck sat silently for a moment, fighting back the stinging

tears that threatened to escape from her eyes and run down her cheeks. She blinked rapidly several times, forcing the tears back.

"Beck? Did you hear me? I said—"

"I heard you." She sniffed hard and rubbed her nose. "Anything else?"

"No."

"Then if you don't mind, I'll get back to the fucking mission then, shall I?" She flicked a middle finger salute up towards the ridge, then rolled to the window where the pocketknife still sat wedged between the frame and the windowsill. She peered through the glass to check that the children were all still asleep, then she gently jiggled the blade until the latch quietly clicked. The sash lifted an inch.

They were in.

Beck motioned to Velasquez, who silently made her way along the balcony to join her. As soon as Velasquez arrived, Beck slid the window up and carefully poked a leg through the gap. She did a passing impression of a talented limbo dancer and squeezed under the upper portion of the window, dropping to the floor. She stood and moved to one side, melting back into the shadows, giving Velasquez room to follow.

She climbed carefully through the window, but as her boot touched the floor it slipped. Velasquez scrabbled for grip and watched as the pocketknife dislodged from the latch and fell in slow motion towards the floor. The tip hit and bounced, clattering, ringing as the metal made contact with the hard surface a second time. Velasquez slid through the window in a heartbeat, and caught the knife as it went for a third strike. She froze, her arm outstretched, the knife in her hand and her eyes locked with Beck's. She mouthed "Sorry" to Beck, who simply held up a clenched fist.

Several of the children stirred. Velasquez held her pose like a statue, screwing her eyes shut as the effort of staying still in a superhero landing pose with one arm stretched out rigid started to make her muscles burn.

The children settled, and Beck glanced to the heavens, rolling her eyes. She looked over at Velasquez and nodded towards the door.

Velasquez stood and moved soundlessly past Beck towards the door. As she passed her friend, she handed her the pocketknife and gave Beck an apologetic smile.

Beck put the knife back in her pocket and looked down the two rows of cots. Cathy was here. She could feel it. She stalked down the middle, glancing at each cot as she passed.

There she was.

Beck froze. She felt like her legs would give out from under her any second. Her breathing stopped and she felt a crushing weight descend onto her chest. She could almost feel her heart breaking.

Cathy lay fast asleep in the end cot. The sleep was deeper than it should have been. It was almost as if the children had been drugged.

Beck motioned to Velasquez, and then pointed at the bottom of Cathy's sleeping bag. Carefully, the two women lifted her off the cot, still wrapped in her sleeping bag. She didn't stir.

They made it to the window, taking baby steps to keep any sound down to an absolute minimum. At the window, Carver waited, his arms outstretched and ready to take the sleeping child. Velasquez carefully handed the end of the sleeping bag over to Carver, and he started to duck-walk back. The tip of the bag shifted in his hands, and he gripped tighter, making sure that Cathy's lower body stayed in the same position.

Just as his wrists passed over the sill, the raised sash dropped with such force that the glass shattered on impact. Carver managed to choke back a scream as it hit both wrists and he stumbled backwards.

Beck watched in horror as Carver let go of Cathy's feet and disappeared from the window. The blood from his wrists glistened in the moonlight. She saw Cathy's feet hit the floor with a thump and knew that all their subterfuge had been blown right out the shattered window, along with any hope of getting Cathy away without disturbing the other children.

She gave Velasquez a desperate look and mouthed "Help me" at her friend. Velasquez shook her head and pointed over Beck's shoulder. Beck, still holding onto Cathy, slowly turned her head. "Oh, shit."

In the middle of the room, the other five children stood, ramrod straight, eyes glowing. As one, they opened their mouths, and a multitude of voices, thousands strong, spoke in unison.

"WE'VE BEEN WAITING FOR YOU."

"This cannot be good." Velasquez braced for impact as the children rushed towards them.

At that moment, Cathy emerged from the sleeping bag, her face drawn back into a snarl and sharp little fingernails swiping and slashing at Beck's face.

"No you don't," Beck said as she grabbed the top of the sleeping bag and hauled it upwards, sending Cathy squealing and thrashing into the foot end. She bunched the top together and with a grunt, swung the bag around in a low arc. The impact knocked the five demon-possessed children off their feet like bowling pins.

"Get that window clear." Beck came around for another swing as two of the children staggered to their feet. The second impact sent them spinning across the floor.

Velasquez punched out the last few shards of glass with her elbow and hopped through. She glanced at Carver. "Okay?"

"Manageable." Carver winced, trying to cover up the fresh gashes on both wrists. Luckily, the cuts hadn't gone too deep and although there was plenty of blood, Carver wasn't in danger of bleeding out any time soon.

Beck was still inside and using bagged-and-tagged Cathy as a scythe to take out the legs of any demon child that tried to get upright. She rotated and lifted the bag up, throwing the bundle towards the window, like a hammer thrower releasing on the final spin. "INCOMING."

Bagged-and-tagged Cathy sailed through the window and into Carver's waiting arms. He caught the child expertly and held the end closed while Velasquez zip-tied it shut.

"GO. GO." Beck sprinted towards the window.

"Look out." Velasquez yelled a warning, but it was too late. The five demon children leapt onto Beck, swarming her, forcing her to the floor. Beck struggled and fought back, but they regrouped and attacked again, demonstrating far more physical strength than the average nine-year-old would normally have.

Beck, a look of grim determination on her face, locked eyes with Velasquez. "GO. Get her to Gabriel. NOW."

"I won't leave you." Velasquez reached out a hand. "Grab my hand."

"Get the fuck out of here, now. That's an order, Velasquez." She paused and gave Velasquez a smile. "I'll be right behind you." She shooed Velasquez and then turned back to fend off another wave of tiny terror attacks from the demon children.

The dormitory door started to shake as someone on the other side pounded at it. A muffled voice yelled at the kids to open the door. Velasquez threw one last desperate look at Beck and vanished. Beck could hear them struggling with the writhing, squirming sleeping bag as they man-handled her daughter down the steps. She snarled and then let out a scream, fighting off the demon children with a renewed vigor. One kid got an elbow in the face. Another got punted across the room as Beck's boot connected with her ass. A third child ended up spinning across the floor and coming to a stop underneath one of the cots, before letting out a bellow and leaping towards Beck on all fours, like a galloping hound. The little fuckers wouldn't quit.

Outside, Velasquez and Carver made their way down the building one balcony at a time. Over the comms, Gabriel's voice sounded sharp. "Someone talk to me. What is going on?"

"Get your holy water ready, we're coming in hot." Carver let out a whoof as Cathy kicked hard, catching him in the ribs.

"We've got Cathy. We're on our way to you." Velasquez's voice almost broke. She handed the still-kicking bundle down to Carver and then followed him.

"What about Beck?"

"She's kinda busy now." Velasquez paused and looked at the third-floor balcony, listening to one hell of a fight. She spoke quickly. "Beck, you hear me? You okay?"

"I said I'm right behi—oof, you little shit. Go. Get Cathy outta here."

In the third-floor dormitory, Beck managed to send another one of the demon children spinning through the air. Momentarily free of their grasping, slashing little hands, she picked up a cot and held it legs out. The children were between her and the window.

She had to time this right or the momentum would take her through the window, over the balcony and straight down. From three floors up, the landing would probably not be a good one. Beck roared and charged the children, the cot held out like a four-legged battering ram. She made contact with the children and through sheer force of will, pushed them backwards. As they impacted the wall by the open window, she flipped, vaulted over the top of the cot and the grasping demon children, and sailed out through the window.

Her judgement was ever-so slightly off, and she found herself hanging by one arm from the third-floor balcony. "Shit." Her climbing skills kicked in and she let go, reaching out and grabbing the second-floor balcony on the way down. It took timing and nerves of steel. But she'd done a drop and grab a thousand times before. The second-floor balcony shook as she made contact, but it held. The ground was too far to risk a superhero landing that might result in a twisted ankle. She did another drop-and-grab to the first floor and let her grip slide easily as she made the final descent.

Beck landed and glared at Carver and Velasquez. "Why are you still here?"

Velasquez grabbed Beck's face with both hands and planted a kiss firmly on her lips. She grinned. "Wasn't going nowhere without you."

A wailing siren sounded. Floodlights pinged on, filling the yard with blazing white light. Velasquez gave Beck a quick smile. "Okay, so this is us, leaving." She shoved Carver and the three started running for the exit point. Carver hoisted the still kicking bagged-and-tagged Cathy in her sleeping bag over one shoulder and put on a burst of speed. They had seconds to make it to the gap. And right now, they were lit up like a fucking mall on Christmas Eve.

The door at the side of the mine office building burst open and three guards sprinted out. The first one made contact with Carver's booby-trapped arbor and hit the floor hard, his gun spinning away from his fingers. The guard's partners piled up behind the prone figure, all crashing to the ground.

The fourth man out of the mine office wasn't so clumsy. Pete sprinted out of the office doorway, yelling. "Stay down." The three guards flattened themselves on the floor, and Pete vaulted over the top of them. As he sailed across the Three Stooges, he brought his AR-15 up, sighted onto Carver and curled his finger around the trigger.

Beck saw the nose of the AR-15 adjust.

Shit.

SHIT.

She had two options. Try to hit Pete or put Carver out of harm's way. She gritted her teeth and took the shot.

Carver dropped, blood seeping into his trousers from a flesh wound on the thigh. It stung like a motherfucker.

But the bullet from Pete's AR-15 that punched through the air where his head had been a second earlier probably would've hurt a whole lot more. Briefly, anyway.

As Beck took the shot, Velasquez brought her own weapon online. She aimed in front of the still-airborne Pete and squeezed the trigger. The bullet hit the guard plate on the AR-15, sending up a cluster of sparks. Pete swore as the gun was knocked out of his grasp. She flipped the gun's setting to auto and yelled. "Covering fire. Move." She opened with an arc of bullets, sending Pete and the guards diving for any cover they could find.

"GO." Beck sprinted towards Carver. She scooped him up, hauling him and the still-bagged Cathy along with her. Velasquez kept up the pressure, firing short, sharp bursts at anything that even thought about moving. Splinters from the window frame, doors and wooden walls filled the air, embedding themselves in any exposed flesh like little daggers. Windows exploded into razor-sharp shards of glass, adding to the general world of hurt that Pete and the guards found themselves living in, keeping them pinned down.

As Beck made for the open compound, the ground started popping in front of her. Puffs of dust indicated where the cascading bullets were landing. She skidded to a stop and then retreated out of range.

"Sniper." She looked up at the third-floor balcony where Bobbi stood, snarling, and firing with a level of accuracy that no air-headed preppy girl should have.

"You little bitch." Beck glared, lifted her M4 and fired, hitting Bobbi in the shoulder.

The girl yelped and spun, sending her towards the railing. She scrabbled for purchase, but the momentum of the spin sent her pinwheeling over the top of the rail. On the way down she swiped a desperate hand at the rail but missed. Bobbi let out a second yell, this time filled with utter panic as she plummeted down. Beck had been right. A fall from the third-floor balcony wasn't good. Beck could hear Bobbi's neck snapping on impact, and the lifeless girl lay still in front of the mine office.

"Move." Beck yelled and the three ex-soldiers, who had extracted themselves from plenty of firefights over the years, fixed their sights on the fence. Carver ignored the burning pain in his leg, scooped up Cathy in her sleeping bag, and tossed it over his huge shoulders like Krampus kidnapping a naughty kid. They had seconds before the entire camp was filled with Lightbringers determined to make things seriously uncomfortable for the crew.

They made the blind spot in between the main huts and paused, regrouping. Beck looked up towards the ridge. "Gabe, how are we looking?"

"We've got movement in the main guard hut."

"No shit, Sherlock." Velasquez winced. "Sorry that came over a bit passive-aggressive, didn't it?"

"Understandable. Looks like they're mustering. One guy giving out guns like candy at Halloween. I would advise immediate egress." He paused. "Is Carver okay?"

"Just a flesh wound, brother. And when I find out who put it there, I'll batter the son of a bitch because it hurts like a motherfucker."

"So you don't know it was B—"

"We're moving." Beck interrupted Gabriel mid-sentence.

Carver raised an eyebrow. "You shot me?"

Beck shrugged. "I'll apologize later. Gabe, guide us through."

"Copy. Okay, hold... hold... okay, move now."

The team crab scuttled towards the hut, then to the head frame. They dropped in behind a pile of crates and paused.

"Hold. Shit. Hostiles, three o'clock."

Beck turned to her left and opened up on a gaggle of Lightbringers heading towards them. They dived out of the way as bullets sang through the air. The searchlights lit up the scene like a Broadway show, working to Beck's advantage. She was good, but she was no Velasquez when it came to marksmanship. She still managed to make at least half a dozen shots count, going for woundings rather than kills because Gabriel's words were ringing in her head. *"We've all made mistakes. You can't deny that. I mean, what's a bigger mistake than murder?"*

She gritted her teeth again and fired, this time dropping two Lightbringers in quick succession with a rapid double-tap.

"Nice shootin' Tex." Velasquez grinned at Beck and picked off two more Lightbringers. "But getting out of here needs to happen real soon. We're getting low on ammo." She reloaded and fired off another burst.

"Time for some diversions." Beck nodded to Carver. "Bud? Make lots of things go bang, would you?"

Carver glared at her. "I still can't believe you shot me."

"Time and place. Light it up."

Carver grinned. "Always a pleasure." He pulled the remote detonator from a pocket, flipped up the red cover and yelled. "Fire in the hole."

There was a whooshing sound and the first batch of fifty-five-gallon drums—full to the brim with gasoline and wired with enough C4 to get the party started—went up. The mushroom cloud blossomed and sent everyone diving for cover. In the dormitory, the demon children screamed as the flames shot up, filling the room with smoke and superheated air. They scrambled towards the door, beating a tattoo with tiny fists until a Lightbringer unlocked it and let them out, chocking and coughing.

"That's our cue." Beck shoved Carver. "Get Cathy to the fence. I'll cover you." She deftly caught the spare magazine Velasquez tossed to her and shoved it in her belt.

"Gabe, are we a go?"

"Affirmative. Go now."

The team, complete with bagged-and-tagged Cathy, sprinted to the next cover point, taking out snipers and Lightbringers along the way. The compound was beginning to fill up with groaning, wounded Lightbringers, punctuated with a series of secondary explosions as the gasoline tanks sent flaming liquid spilling across the compound.

They made the second pause point, another stack of fifty-five-gallon drums with yet another of Carver's sparks attached. "We do not want to be here any longer than we have to." Carver looked serious for a second.

"Why not?"

Carver looked sheepish. "I might've put a bit too much C4 on this one." He shrugged.

"As in?"

"A block and a half?"

"Fuck's sake, you'll take out half the damn compound."

"And that's a bad thing, why, exactly?"

Beck paused and then nodded. "Fair point. We good?"

"In three, two, one, GO."

The team moved out of the hot zone towards the fence.

The Lightbringer was huge.

And in the way.

And very, very angry.

Beck skidded to a halt, raised the gun, and pointed it straight at him and without taking her eyes off the huge man, shouted to Velasquez. "I'll be right behind you. Keep going." She fired a single round at the Lightbringer, hitting him in the shoulder. He jerked sideways, glanced down at the thin line of blood that trickled from his shoulder, and refocused on Beck.

She snarled. "Seriously?" Beck fired again, hitting his other shoulder. Again, the Lightbringer merely twitched and kept stalking towards her, eyes glowing, face twisted into an ugly grimace. Beck repositioned her hands and sighed. Time to break another promise. "Sorry." She opened up on the Lightbringer, punching bullet after bullet into him.

The Lightbringer ignored the swarm of bullets, twitching and jerking but still relentlessly moving towards him. Beck emptied the clip, jettisoned it, reloaded. "Oh, c'mon." She brought the gun up and started firing again.

"He's a sentinel. Get out of there now."

"A what?" Beck fired another shot at the bastard out of spite and backed up.

"A sentinel. They guard the gates of Hell itself. They're almost impossible to kill."

Beck kept backing away, firing single shots. "Quantify almost impossible."

"Ever tried shooting a rhino?"

"Yeah, and now I can never go to the zoo again. What the fuck are you talking about?" Beck popped another bullet into the sentinel.

"Think zombies. Body shots won't do anything to stop a sentinel. You need to aim for his eye. Make it count, though, the bullet has to go right through the middle."

There was a pop from behind Beck's shoulder. The sentinel's eye exploded in a spray of vitreous fluid and blood. He roared and dropped to his knees.

"Like that?" Velasquez lowered her gun and grinned.

"Yes, exactly like that."

Beck turned her back on the sentinel as the glow in his one remaining eye finally winked out and he toppled forward face first into the dust. She started to walk away past one of the shafts that dotted the compound.

The wet, tearing sound and long, low, rolling growl stopped her in her tracks. She turned slowly, eyes widening in disbelief.

The sentinel's human form had been ripped in two. The remains were currently spreadeagled on the dirt like a Viking Blood Eagle. The blood-covered hellhound stood in the bloody detritus and drew its lips back revealing a lot more teeth than the average German Shepherd. They were longer. Sharper. Dripping with venom. And above this mouthful of death glowed two red eyes filled with utter evil.

The hellhound padded forward, the growl growing with every step. The hound's snout wrinkled, and it pulled its lips back even further.

"Oh, shit." Beck swung up the M4 and aimed.

The hound leapt. Powerful back legs sent the beast hurtling into the air. It slammed into Beck, sending the M4 spinning out of her hands. "FUCK." Beck wrestled with the beast, grabbing the thick fur around its neck, and holding the snapping jaws at arm's length. She stumbled towards the shaft and scrabbled for balance for a split second. With a huge grunt, she flung her arms over her head, sending the hound arcing over the top of her and into the shaft. As the beast toppled into the abyss, she tried to let go, but her balance had gone beyond that critical point. With a shriek, Beck fell backwards into the shaft and vanished from view.

"BECK!" Velasquez screamed as she saw Beck disappear. She lunged forward but Carver grabbed her by the arm.

"No. There's nothing we can do." Carver wrestled with the distraught woman for a second. "We have to go now."

Velasquez, tears in her eyes, took one last look at the shaft, hoping, wishing, praying that by some miracle Beck's head would pop back into view.

With a final sob wracking her body, she turned and ran after Carver.

They made the fence, pushed the sleeping bag with Cathy in it through the hole and climbed through. Velasquez squatted by the fence and looked at Carver. Her eyes were filled with grief and fury. "Light those motherfuckers up."

Carver, his expression grim and full of anger, nodded. He flipped the detonator and pushed the button. The second explosion made the first one look like a party popper. It rocked the entire compound, sending Lightbringers into the air and crashing back down again. The cries and moans of the dying filled the night.

Velasquez stared at the carnage. "Motherfuckers."

Carver placed a gentle hand on her shoulder. "Let's go."

Velasquez looked one last time at the mineshaft, still hoping in her heart to see Beck emerge bloodied but alive. She felt Carver pull at her and finally tore her gaze away from the shaft, following her friend and their package into the darkness.

In the compound, Pete, flanked by a dozen grim-faced Lightbringers, surrounded the mine shaft. He stared into the darkness. "She's down there."

"Sir, she wouldn't have survived the drop."

Pete turned to the Lightbringer and stared at him, his eyes glowing. "You don't know her like I do." He turned to the rest of the group. "Half of you with me. The rest of you, go after her friends and get my daughter back." He shouted to the Lightbringers who had survived the blast. "And put those damn fires out." Pete turned his attention to the mineshaft and snarled. "Bitch." He fired randomly into the shaft. Even if the bitch was already dead, he wanted to put a bullet in her to make sure. The round ricocheted off the stone and hit the metal surface of a skip about ten feet down, sending sparks cascading into the darkness. "BITCH." Pete stamped off with half a dozen Light-bringers following in his wake, shouting orders at any Light-bringer still capable of standing.

In the mineshaft and safely hidden away from the bullet with her name on it, Beck swung in the darkness, holding on to a strut sticking out from the side of the shaft. The skip shielded her from view. She swung onto the skip, crouching, and clicked the comms. "Vel, you hear me?"

Velasquez's voice sounded in her earpiece. Beck? BECK? You're alive."

"Yeah, but not for much longer if I don't get outta here. Listen. You've got six Lightbringers on your ass. A couple look like they might be those sentinels too, big sons of bitches. I'm gonna try and get out of here before Pete and his pets show up."

"I'm coming for you."

"No. I told you, you've got six Lightbringers on your tail. I'll head down and across to the west shaft. There's a secondary tunnel that leads to an exit near the highway. About a click west from the gate. Meet me there. If I'm not with you in thirty minutes, go. And sweetie?"

"Yes?"

Beck paused. "Don't look back, okay? Without Cathy, we stop these bastards and their end of the world shit. You gotta think of the bigger picture. You understand?"

"But—"

"I said, do you understand?"

Silence. Then Velasquez's voice came over, small and lost. "I understand."

"Good."

"Beck?"

"Yes?"

"I love you."

Beck smiled in the darkness. "I love you too. Now go. And I'll see you in thirty."

In the scrubland away from the compound, Velasquez felt a tear slide down her cheek. She glanced at Carver. "Tell me you put a third-time-lucky in that fucking compound."

Carver nodded. "You know me. I'm nothing if not thorough." He flipped a detonator switch, and a third explosion sent the headframe crashing to the ground, twisted metal taking out two huts and half of the mine office on the way. More screams filled the night air as the Lightbringers discovered what Hell really felt like, courtesy of Carver and his stash of C4.

The two soldiers watched as the fireball engulfed three of the six Lightbringers bottlenecked at the fence. Their screams echoed through the darkness. Velasquez locked eyes with one and watched serenely as his burning fingers gripped the chain link fence and the flames swirled around his body. She held up her hand and waved bye-bye to the screaming man.

Without taking her eyes away from the carnage, she spoke to Carver. "How much C4 did you use?"

He shrugged. "All of it?" He hoisted Cathy onto his back. "We better get moving."

36

In the chaos of the compound, Pete stood, an island of calm in a fiery maelstrom. Pastor Reid strolled towards him with the five demon children trailing behind like a comet tail. He walked up to Pete and studied him with a quizzical look. "Your ex-wife?"

"Who else?"

Pastor Reid sighed. "She is becoming a bit of a problem."

Pete nodded towards the shaft. "She went down there. With one of your hellhounds."

Pastor Reid chuckled. "So, she's already on her way to Hell, then. Good."

Pete rested the AR-15 on his shoulder and shook his head. "Your puppy may be on its way to a warm basket and a demonic chew toy by the fires of Hades, but you don't know Beck like I do. She's still alive. I can feel it. The bitch is harder to kill than a cockroach. Believe me, I've tried more than once."

"Well, then I suggest you get down there and check that our little cockroach hasn't fucked up what we've done, don't you think?"

Pete nodded. "We're on it. We're waiting for the power."

"Power?" Pastor Reid leaned forward until his face was inches from Pete's. His eyes lit up, a swirling mass of blinding light. As Pete stared into Reid's eyes, the light seemed to fill his entire world. He could see the faces of the damned twisting and screaming silently in agony. Reid's voice oozed through the vision, like poisoned honey. "Have I taught you nothing, Pete? You're a Lightbringer. You don't need manmade power to see into the heart of the darkness. Have I not given you all the true power you need? Or do you feel my gifts are not enough?"

With a blink, the vision was gone, and Pastor Reid straightened, smiling benignly at Pete. "Now go. Hunt your little cockroach down. And Pete?"

Pete tried to stop his heart from exploding with fear. He shook visibly as he raised his eyes to look once more at Pastor Reid. "Yes, my lord?"

"Do me a little favor and kill the bitch this time, understood?"

Pete bowed his head. As he brought his head back up, his eyes blazed, and he smiled slowly. "Yes, my lord."

37

Gabriel sat on the ridge, watching the whole shitshow unfold in front of him. The third-time-lucky explosion took him by surprise with the sheer ferocity of the blast. He ripped the night-vision scope away from his arm before the flare burnt out his retina. "You lunatic." He didn't need a scope to see the mushroom cloud bloom towards the sky. They'd probably seen that in Oregon.

A scrabbling sound to his left made him start and he

grabbed an iron bar with his right hand, ready to swing. A low whistle made him relax his grip. A second later, Carver and Velasquez appeared, carrying the unconscious Cathy still balled up in her sleeping bag.

Wordlessly, Carver cut the tie and unzipped the bag. Cathy rolled out and lay motionless on the dirt. He stood back. "Looks almost sweet, lying there, doesn't she?"

"Don't be fooled. Cathy isn't our enemy. It's what's inside her that we need to fear." Gabriel crouched and checked her pulse. It was steady, if a little quick. He stood and nodded. "She's unharmed. Let's get her to the motel."

Carver's eyes widened. "Are you nuts? We need to get that demon or whatever the hell it is out of her now."

Gabriel shook his head. "Even your pyrotechnics aren't going to hold them forever."

"I dunno. We did some serious damage down there. There are a lot fewer Lightbringers now than there were this time yesterday."

Gabriel shook his head again. "They are Legion. Remember that. You kill one, two take its place. Besides, we're on the clock here to rendezvous with Beck." He looked at his watch. "Twenty-three minutes and counting."

A puff of dirt next to Cathy's head made them all look up sharply. Velasquez aimed down the slope and unleashed a swarm of bullets towards the scrub. "And that's our signal to get the fuck out of here, guys." She fired another burst into the darkness. "So stop screwing around, get the kid, and let's go."

Carver scooped up Cathy in his arms and tossed her over his shoulder like a bag of coal. Gabriel gathered up his scope and rucksack and the team made tracks away from the ridge, trying to ignore the disturbing and distinctly canine snuffling sounds from the scrub.

Velasquez scowled. "Oh, I fucking hate hellhounds. Hang on a second, guys."

"We don't have time." Gabriel turned.

"Make time, okay? Give me a second." Velasquez took up a sniper position and slowed her breathing. She reached into her pack and pulled out three shining silver bullets.

Carver frowned. "That's for werewolves."

"Not when the fucker's been dipped in Holy Water, they're not. Silver will take out a hellhound too, and basically any denizen of Hell as long as you get the son of a bitch right in the heart." She glanced at Gabriel. "Or in the eye?" He nodded and she smiled. "Now shut the fuck up and let me concentrate." She looked through the scope and scanned the scrub. The snuffling got louder. Seventy-five yards. Sixty-five yards.

Fifty yards.

Velasquez closed her eyes, and felt the blissful silence wrap itself around her. It always happened this way—just before a perfect shot. She smiled, opened one eye, lined up the crosshairs, and gently squeezed the trigger.

A yelp in the bushes told her she'd hit her target. She moved the barrel a couple of degrees left, fired again, moved the business end of the gun right, and fired a third shot. Three thuds told her she'd hit the hound and the two sentinels perfectly— the hound in the heart and the two sentinels right through the eye.

She sat back, flipped the safety on and looked at the two men. "Now we can go." She stood and slung the rifle over her shoulder. She gave the scrub one last look and muttered. "I fucking hate hellhounds."

38

There are no words to describe how black the bottom of a mineshaft really is. It has substance. Dimensions. You can reach out and grab a handful, squeeze it, and feel the blackness running between your fingers and down your arm.

So the fact that the bottom of this mineshaft was as bright as a fitted kitchen with all the lights on took Beck back a little. The climb down from the skip had been one of the most challenging of Beck's life. But she'd night-climbed plenty of times and had learned to trust her instincts when her fingers were inching across jagged rocks, probing, searching for grip holds. As her eyes became accustomed to the darkness, the surface of the shaft began to emerge, and the climb became easier.

Then the power came on, and light flooded up the shaft. That made the last fifty feet or so a damn sight easier.

She landed like a cat and dusted her hands on her combats. She glanced around and started. "Jesus."

The hellhound's body lay crumpled on the floor. It was still twitching, the huge paws paddling at the air and the ribcage convulsing and shuddering. Beck unsheathed her knife and pulled out a small bottle from her backpack. She flipped open the lid, poured holy water along the blade and then plunged the knife into the hound. The hound's body stiffened and then erupted into white flames, burning to ash in seconds.

Beck watched the creature head straight to the dog basket that awaited it in Hell. She popped the cap on the bottle and tucked it back into the backpack. The knife nestled back into its sheath, and Beck pulled out a small compass. She stared down the horizontal tunnel, watching the string of lightbulbs flicker and then stabilize. "Huh. No need for a torch, then." She smiled and took one step forward.

A skittering sound from above made her stop and look up.

Staring back down at her from the shaft walls were five sets of eyes, glowing in the gloom. A hissing, chattering noise filled the tunnel, bouncing off the stone walls and filtering down to Beck. "Oh no."

At the entrance to the shaft, Pastor Reid smiled as he watched the children scuttle down the walls of the shaft like geckos. "Suffer the children, unbeliever. Suffer the children."

Beck watched the possessed children skitter and scrabble on all fours, their glowing eyes never once breaking their mesmerizing gaze. Beck snapped out of her frozen state as a rock dislodged by one of the children bounced its way down the shaft and landed next to her. "Fuck this." She set off at a fast jog down the tunnel. There was no point in wasting time looking back. She knew the children were swarming and clambering their way along the shaft and down to the tunnel in pursuit. She didn't want to kill them. They were kids. But she knew damn well that if they caught up with her, there would be no quarter given. She ran on, her boots slamming into the dirt floor and sending up clouds of dust. She needed to get the hell out of Dodge, and fast. Before Pete and his gun-toting pals teamed up with the demon kids and decided to kick her ass once and for all.

In the distance, she heard the whine of a motor start up and a rumble as the skip trundled its way down the shaft. "Shit. Shit." Beck accelerated, following the twists and turns of the tunnel, knowing that behind her, Hell was unleashing everything it had.

39

Carver and Gabriel paused at the edge of the south ridge. They'd made it to the rope. "You see her?"

Gabriel peered into the bushes, his night-vision scope penetrating the darkness and creating a lime green world where every detail shone out. "Yeah, she's with us."

Velasquez skidded to a halt and slumped down beside her friends. "We got company."

"Shit, not more hellhounds?" Carver scowled.

"Nah. These are all human. About three of them. Crashing around like mad. Skilled hunters they ain't." She nodded towards the lump in the sleeping bag. "She okay?"

"She's fine. Probably pretty pissed, but fine." Carver shrugged.

"We need to get moving." Velasquez checked her rifle. "We've got no more than two, maybe three minutes and we'll have one hell of a firefight on our hands."

Carver looked at Velasquez. "You okay?"

"I'm fine." Velasquez grimly cocked the rifle and flicked the safety off.

"You sure?"

"I said I'm fine. Don't ask me again." She stood. "We ready?"

Gabriel nodded. "Carver, you okay to keep hold of Cathy?"

Carver picked up the sleeping bag and pulled out a knife. He cut two holes in the bag and threaded a length of webbing through it. Securing the webbing, he slung the bag across his shoulders like a backpack. "I'm good."

Dropping the belay device over the edge of the ridge, he looked at his friends. "See you at the bottom." He hooked up and repelled into the darkness.

Velasquez watched him drop and then nodded to Gabriel. "You're up."

"You first."

"Don't fucking argue. You're not exactly the one to hold them off at the pass if the walking dead turn up, are you, mister I'll-never-hold-a-gun-again? Now get the fuck down that rope." Velasquez shoved Gabriel towards the anchor point. "Move."

"Promise me one thing before I hook up."

"What?"

Gabriel placed a gentle hand on her shoulder. "That you're not going to try some stupid rescue mission and go back for Beck."

Velasquez glared at Gabriel. "How stupid do you think I am, monk? I know this whole thing is bigger than any of us. Yes, it hurts knowing Beck is gone. My God, it hurts so bad. But if we don't get that kid out of here, we'll all be joining her, and thousands, even millions of others will die too." She took a step forward, her face inches from Gabriel's. "These whackadoodles ain't Waco wannabes. They want to bring the antichrist into existence. They wanna watch the world burn." She stepped back and sighed. "And I'm not gonna let that happen. Not even if it meant a chance to save Beck." Her shoulders dropped. "So don't worry. Okay? Now hook up and get the fuck down that rope."

Gabriel hooked up and smiled at her. "See you down there."

Velasquez nodded.

Gabriel launched himself over the edge of the ridge and Velasquez turned back, ready to make things interesting for anyone stupid enough to come after them. She could hear the shushing sound of his belay device as it sped down the rope.

A crack in the undergrowth grabbed her attention as a twig snapped underneath a foot. Velasquez grinned, raised the rifle, and sang quietly. "Come out, come out, wherever you are."

Carver hit the bottom of the ravine with a thud. His injured leg sent a shockwave of pain up through his torso and he gasped. "Son of a bitch."

"You okay?" Gabriel's voice floated down.

"Yeah, I'm good. Just, shit, why did she have to shoot me in the damn leg?" Carver grimaced and shifted his weight. He unhooked and stepped out of the way as Gabriel landed. "Where's Vel?"

A burst of gunfire ripped through the night air. The random shooting was punctuated with the throaty, deeper sound of Velasquez's rifle efficiently double tapping. Carver and Gabriel pressed themselves against the wall of the ravine, keeping clear of any stray ricochets that might ping their way. Gabriel glanced up. "She's still up there."

A swooshing sound filled the air, followed by another burst of gunfire. The rope vibrated and Velasquez appeared out of the darkness, repelling with one hand, and firing up towards the ridge with the other. "I'm coming in hot. They're right behind me." She bounced to a stop and swung her feet down. Gabriel shot forward and unhooked her while she kept firing up towards the ridge. "They've got friends. There's a whole swarm of the fuckers up there. We need to go now." She fired again. "They're using our own damn rope. Move, move."

Gabriel pointed to the river. "Get going. I'll take care of this."

Carver and Velasquez nodded and sprinted towards the river.

Gabriel unsheathed his Ka-Bar and watched as one of the shooters slid down the rope using his AR-15 as a belay. "Clever." He waited until the shooter was half-way down, and then cut the base of the rope away from the piton. He grabbed the loose end and yanked it hard. The rope pinged, and the shooter's feet slipped. He scrabbled wildly at the rope, sending the AR-15 clattering down the cliff-face.

Gravity made a guest appearance.

The man let out a single scream and fell, flailing wildly all the way down.

Gabriel turned away as the man hit the ground. Blood splattered up, spraying Gabriel and the cliff wall. He turned back, made the sign of the cross over the man's crumpled body, and ran.

40

Beck, still very much alive and increasingly angry, pounded through the tunnel. She leapt over debris and broken support beams. The skittering sound grew closer and closer. The heat sucked the energy out of muscles that had been asked to do way too much in the past few days. She could feel the sting of lactic acid hitting her system, sapping the strength out of her legs.

Desperation started to kick in. She'd been in some shitty

positions before. That was the nature of the job. You play stupid games with Hell, you win stupid prizes. You trade bullets with the devil, you end up getting hurt. That fucker's a good shot. Almost as good as Beck.

Almost.

But not quite.

Beck dug deep. She found the reserve all soldiers have. The little bit in the bottom of the tank that can mean the difference between surviving and dying. That little burst of spiritual pep-up-pill that gets you to the escape point and out the other side.

If she survived the night, she'd be flat on her back recovering for a week, that was for damn sure. Old war wounds reminded her of past mistakes. The ever-present ache of her scars dialed up to a dull roar.

She heard Gabriel's voice in her mind. "Use the pain. Capture it. Condense it. Use it to fire you on."

Ignoring every screaming muscle, every zing of lactic acid, every doubt and every bitter memory, Beck ran on.

41

The fence loomed in front of them. Carver, Gabriel, and Velasquez crouched by the chain links. Velasquez reached into a pocket and swore. "Crap. I've lost the cutters."

"No need. The entrance to the east shaft is over there. Clear run. We get into the shaft, and it's a short run out the other side." Gabriel pointed. "We're almost there." They scuttled along the fence to the entrance and, one at a time, dipped into the darkness. Gabriel clicked on a flashlight and swept the entrance. "Struts are gone, so we're gonna need to watch for cave-ins." He pointed the beam down. "Rails are still there, though."

"Better than fucking breadcrumbs." Carver grinned.

"I'll take point. Stay behind me." Velasquez, grim-faced and serious, flipped down her night-vision goggles and stepped into the gloom.

"You heard the lady." Carver pointed at the entrance, and Gabriel followed Velasquez into the gloom.

Carver gave one last glance behind to make sure they weren't being followed and ducked into the shaft. They were nearly out. Not much further now.

42

The skip wheels shrieked to a stop at the bottom of the shaft, the noise echoing down through the tunnels and into the depths of the mine. Pete punched the "STOP" button and the skip juddered to a halt. He turned on his headlight and smiled. Cupping a hand around his mouth, he called out. "Rebecca. Coming. Ready or not." The smile turned nasty. "REBECCA. I'm coming for you." Pete opened the gate and stepped into the tunnel. In a sing-song voice, he called out again. "REBECCA. Where are you?" He chuckled. Turning to his colleagues, he motioned them down the tunnel. He could see her footprints in the dust.

Let the hunt begin.

Ahead, Beck heard Pete's voice floating through the air. So now she knew where he was. Behind the kids. At least they hadn't doubled around and cut her off via the east shaft. With any luck, the team would already be there, using the shaft as a fast get-out-of-town route to the truck. All she had to do now was find her way to the east shaft exit and she was home and dry.

She skidded to a halt at a T-junction. She scowled as she desperately tried to visualize the twists and turns on the map back in the visitor center. Left or right? Left or right?

Right. Go right. She ran down the right tunnel and around a corner. Another few yards and she skidded to a stop. "Shit. Shit, shit, shit." a solid rockface blocked her path. Beck had no option. She had to turn back and take the left tunnel. And she had to do it before those damn demon children and Pete showed up. She started to jog towards the T-junction.

The lights flickered and the tunnel was filled with a chittering, hissing sound. "Oh, fuck no." Beck turned to see one of the demon children walking slowly and purposefully around the corner. The child stopped about twenty-five yards away and stood, simply staring. The other four children scuttled along the walls and ceiling, their heads pivoting around impossibly to stare at Beck. The tunnel was completely blocked.

"I don't want to hurt you." Beck felt the tears sting her eyes. Not kids. She didn't want to have to kill kids, for Chrissake. She lifted the M4 and flicked the safety to off. "Please. Don't come any closer. I'm begging you. I don't want to hurt you."

The demon child slowly smiled, and a little chuckle echoed around the tunnel. She mimicked Beck. "Please. I'm begging you. I don't want to hurt you." The child laughed again and as her mouth opened wide the perfect pearly-white teeth elongated into deadly, needle-like daggers.

Beck, shifting her position and bracing her shoulder, blinked away the tears and aimed at that needle-filled maw.

43

The tunnel turned slowly. Velasquez stopped and checked her compass. "This is the one that heads east."

Gabriel shined his flashlight down the tunnel and frowned. "What if it doesn't connect?"

"You were the one that said we were close." Velasquez turned to him and stared. "You telling me you're having a geographical wobble here?"

Gabriel shook his head. "I don't have Beck's eidetic memory."

Velasquez looked at the compass again, watching the swaying needle come to rest. "East will take us towards the truck and away from the compound. So I'm gonna go with east." She snapped the compass shut. "East is good." She glared at Gabriel. "You got any better ideas?"

"We got company." Carver sprinted up to them and spun around, taking a defensive position. "Gabe, you need to take Cathy. Keep going. I'll hold them off."

He shrugged off the makeshift rucksack containing the still motionless Cathy.

"Carver. Grenade." Velasquez reached into a pocket and pulled out a grenade. She tossed it to Carver who caught it in mid-air.

"That'll bring the damn roof down." Gabriel's eyes widened.

"As long as we're on this side and they're on that side, I do not see a problem with that, do you?" Velasquez's eyes were cold and emotionless.

"They're human beings."

"They're fucking Lightbringers. They wanna end the world, remember? And they'll kill kids to do it." Velasquez snarled at Gabriel. "Now pick up Cathy and let's go."

"You heard her, get moving. Don't worry, I'll be right behind you." Carver got into a crouched position, using the corner of the tunnel as cover. He had a good line of sight. Good. But not perfect. If he didn't get it right first time, they'd pin him down until he ran out of bullets.

Carver listened to the retreating footsteps of Gabriel and Velasquez, and then refocused his attention on the tunnel. The clatter of running feet echoed around the rock walls, making it sound like an entire army of Lightbringers were heading his way. He braced, ready to engage down to the last damn bullet. The grenade sat in the dirt next to him. Last resort. A final Hail Mary. The grenade would take everyone out. Lightbringers, demon children, Pete, and his pets, everyone.

Including Carver.

44

Beck's M4 shook. She tried to aim at the leg of the child, but her hand trembled so badly that she simply couldn't hold the line of sight steady.

The child relentlessly stalked towards her, each shuffling step bringing that demonic maw ever closer.

"Rebecca. There you are." Pete walked around the corner, his palms outstretched and a smile on his face. The demon

KRISTEN CROSS & MARK STEENSLAND

child stopped in her tracks, letting Pete move past and in front of her, shielding the child from Beck's M4. "Easy, Rebecca, easy, baby. Put the gun down. There's a good girl." Pete's voice was pure honey. Every word slid into her mind like a greased eel. The strength drained from her arms, and she lowered the gun. Pete's smile locked into place. "There's no way out." Behind him, three more Lightbringers and Pastor Reid clustered into the tunnel. Pete was right. There was no way out.

A lightning bolt of defiance shot through her, and she laughed. "Do what you want with me, you asshole. Nothing matters now. I got Cathy away from you and your sick bastard friends. You're finished."

Pastor Reid snarled. "End this, Pete. End it now."

Pete held up a hand, silencing the Pastor. "Sweetie, it's not us who are sick. It's you. It's always been you." He took a step forward. "All you've been through, all the trauma you suffered fighting for our country?" Another step. "It's bound to have had an effect on you. And we want to help you. We really do." And another step. "Come with us and let us show you the truth. You don't have to be scared of what you don't understand. We'll explain it all. I promise." He held out a hand. "Come with me."

Beck felt a tug on her shirt and glanced down. The five demon children surrounded her, smiling, loving faces turned up towards her, all holding her. She felt a small hand slip into hers. It felt like Cathy's hand.

The M4 rolled in her fingers and clattered onto the ground.

"There you go." Pete took one last step towards Beck and took her still-outstretched hand. She felt his strong fingers winding with hers. The warmth of his palm against hers. Pete. Back in her life. Back in her soul.

She'd missed that. The feeling that despite her always

having to be the strong one, the leader, the fearless soldier, there was someone waiting for her who could make her feel safe. Feel loved. Feel whole.

She'd missed him so much. So much. She closed her eyes and tightened her grip on his hand. His soft voice wrapped itself around her. "Come with us."

The children shepherded her down the tunnel. Pastor Reid smiled, turned, and led the group to the T-junction. He turned to the solid rock wall and ran questioning fingers over the surface. He found what he was looking for and pressed. The wall slid apart to reveal a heavy oak door. Massive iron brackets attached the door to hinges that were anchored into the rock itself. A large keyhole sat on the right of the door. It looked as old as time itself.

Heat radiated from the doorway. Around the frame, a halo of yellow-orange light escaped, sending shafts of light into the tunnel. Dust motes floated in the light, swirling on the eddies of heat that curled through the gap between the wall and the door.

Pastor Reid pulled out a key and slotted it into the keyhole. He turned the lock and a loud click echoed. The door swung open, and a blast of heat and light filled the tunnels.

The children led Beck to the doorway. She looked back at Pete, fear in her eyes. He shook his head and smiled. "Don't worry. It's okay."

Pastor Reid swept his arm dramatically towards the open doorway. "Time to pay the piper, Rebecca."

The children, in a voice that sounded like a thousand souls screaming, spoke as one. "MALPHAS IS WAITING."

Realization hit home. Hard. Beck snapped out of the walking coma Pete's honeyed voice had sent her into and screamed. She tried to back away, but the children had formed a solid wall behind her. Ten little hands snatched at her, grabbing her, pushing her forward.

She screamed again. Pete's rolling, growing laughter drowned out her agonized wail, the soft, gentle voice now long gone, replaced by the amusement of the devil himself.

45

The scream ripped through the tunnels, bouncing off the walls, distorted by the rockface. The quartz seams grabbed hold of the scream, added a plethora of sharp edges to it and resonated it on. By the time it reached Velasquez and Gabriel, it sounded like a thousand screams from a thousand terrified Becks.

Gabriel slid to a halt. "Beck." He felt a hand grab his sleeve and pull hard.

"The mission." Velasquez's face was grim.

"But—"

"No buts. We've had this conversation already. I ain't having it again. Let's go."

"Vel—"

Velasquez spun him around. She flipped up her night-vision goggles and stared hard into his eyes. "Listen, you ass. You think I don't wanna go charging in to save her? You think it isn't breaking my heart hearing that? Huh? Do you? But if they get their hands on our little precious bundle there, we all die. We get Cathy clear, get you and her in the truck and out of danger, and then I'll go back for Beck. If you want, you can come too. Okay? Are we clear on that?"

Gabriel nodded.

"Good." Velasquez flipped her goggles back into place. "Now pick up the pace, soldier."

They set off at a fast trot. As they came to a bend in the tunnel, Velasquez slammed an arm back, pushing Gabriel into the wall. Her arm snapped up, her fist tightly balled. They froze.

The tunnel connected with a second passageway with a shaft leading down to the next level. A patrol of Lightbringers trotted past. Their eyes glowed in the darkness, showing up as brilliant dots in Velasquez's night vision goggles. Whatever was possessing the Lightbringers didn't need modern technology to see in the gloom. It was doing fine by itself.

The patrol disappeared around another corner. Velasquez waited for another thirty seconds before moving, to make sure the sons of bitches didn't double back. She turned to Gabriel. "The kid okay?"

Gabriel nodded. "It's like a damn parrot. Put a cover over it and whatever that demon is inside her shuts down."

Velasquez sighed. "Shame it couldn't be that simple for those motherfuckers, huh?" She jabbed a thumb towards the tunnel. "Okay. This passage runs north-south. That means we gotta go down and get on an east heading." She held up a hand. "Yeah, I know it's counter-intuitive, but don't forget, that compound was way higher up than the road. We go down, follow it east, and we should pop out at the base of the hill."

"I agree." Gabriel looked down the shaft. "Let me go first this time."

Velasquez nodded and moved aside. Gabriel grasped the ladder bolted to the side of the shaft. It wobbled and creaked. Flakes of rust sloughed off the surface and floated down to the tunnel below. "Looks kinda rickety. Let me get to the bottom first. I don't think it'll take all our weight in one go."

"Just fucking climb, will you?" Velasquez scanned the tunnel for more patrols.

Gabriel braced himself against the ladder and quickly climbed to the tunnel below. He cleared the ladder and let out a low whistle. A quiet shuffling sound told him that Velasquez was already half-way down the ladder by the time his whistle had faded into nothing. He glanced around the tunnel. Next to a support beam sat a white box. Gabriel frowned and moved closer.

Behind him, Velasquez landed with a hop at the bottom of the ladder. She looked around and noticed Gabriel hunched over something. "What you got?"

Gabriel hooked a finger under a wire and held it up. "C4. And lots of it." He turned to Velasquez. "Guess that's what they meant by 'The fire is coming' then, huh?"

"Shit." Velasquez glanced at her watch. "Dawn's in twenty

minutes. We're never gonna make it out of here before this lot goes boom."

Gabriel stood and dusted his hands. "Yes we will." He smiled. "God's on our side."

Velasquez frowned. "Yeah. But does God have C4 and detonator cord on hand?"

46

Carver heard the Lightbringer patrol trot past the tunnel. Shit. Shit. The acoustics in the tunnel had thrown him for a complete loop. They were a level over, the bastards. He repositioned his gun, grabbed the spare clips and grenade that Velasquez had tossed to him, and checked his compass. East. Go east. Follow Velasquez and Carver.

He set off at a jog, the night vision goggles making every

inch of the tunnel shimmer in a fluorescent green. The tunnel bent around and came to a T-junction running north-south. "Damn it." Which way would they have gone? Left? Right? Down? He grinned. Velasquez was like a little terrier when she got going. North would take them deeper into the mountain. South would take them towards the compound. Down would get them on track. He grabbed the rusty ladder and scuttled down, jumping off the last step and turning.

The business end of an M4 was about an inch from the end of his nose. Carver froze.

"You asshole, I nearly blew your fucking head off." Velasquez dropped the M4 and glared at Carver. "You okay?"

"Yeah. That patrol was—"

"—To our side, yeah, we know. Freaky-assed acoustics in this place are messing with us. They went past us by the shaft so they're above us." Velasquez grinned. "You seen this?" She nodded towards Gabriel, who had dismantled the C4 bomb and snipped the wire. Gabriel held up a block of explosive.

"Shit."

"Yeah, and there's a ton more where that came from. Literally. We've looked down the tunnel. There's white boxes full of C4 at every strategic support." Gabriel stood up. "Looks like they mean to bring the whole mountain down."

"When?"

"Dawn."

"Now I know we're in trouble." Carver frowned.

Velasquez gave him a look. "You think?"

"No, not the plastic. I mean, yes, the whole kaboomy, dying in a fiery furnace that leads straight down to hell kinda trouble, obviously."

Gabriel ignored him. "We need to move. We have less than

fifteen minutes before dawn. Getting the kid out of here may have bought us some time, but not much."

Velasquez held up a hand. "Wait. You feel that?"

"What?"

"A breeze." She grinned. We're near the exit. Come on."

The breeze got stronger as they ran towards the exit. As the team got closer, they slowed down. The chances were that at least one Lightbringer was keeping watch over the exit. Velasquez was on point and held up a balled fist. They stopped, waiting for her signal.

Velasquez scanned the exit for guards. She frowned. "Well, I guess they're all at the pre-Armageddon buffet or something because we're clear." She waved them on and through into the clean pre-dawn air. It was cold. Damn cold. But it felt like a Caribbean breeze compared to the stifling heat in the mine.

They could see the dark, boxy outline of the Range Rover in the shadows. Velasquez let a small smile flicker over her lips. "We've made it. We've actually made it." She turned to Carver and Gabriel. "Get the kid in the car and keep the engine running."

Carver frowned. "Where are you going?"

Velasquez turned towards the exit, a grim look on her face. She jettisoned the magazine from the M4, checked it with a tap, and re-inserted it. Full up. One in the bank. She flipped the safety off and glanced back at Carver. "To get Beck."

47

B eck's scream faded into the mountain. Pete chuckled
and followed her into the chamber. Its perfectly
smooth walls and round shape were clearly not the
work of gnarled old timey gold diggers. This was unnatural.
Unholy. Hundreds of candles created a suffocating, smoky heat
haze. A sticky liquid oozed down the walls, adding the tinny,
metallic scent of blood to the mix. The black surface was
covered in orange striations that seemed to bend and twist as

Beck looked at them. Occasionally, a face, its mouth wide open and contorted in agony, tried to push its way through the surface before absorbing back into the blackness. It was as if a thousand agonized souls were trapped inside those black walls, struggling to break free.

In the center of the round chamber was a pit lined with stone blocks. Like a huge well, it spanned at least twenty feet. Clouds of smoke and steam curled upwards, uplit by a violent orange glow. A churning, glooping sound came from the pit, like molasses on a rolling boil.

"Take her." Pastor Reid motioned to the Lightbringers, who grabbed Beck and hauled her towards the pit.

"Wait." Pete held up a hand. He stalked across the chamber and stood face to face with his ex-wife. "I'm giving you one last chance. Join us. Join us before the fire comes. We're offering you freedom."

Beck's face crumpled into a snarl, and she spat into Pete's face, wishing with every fiber in her being that the spittle was filled with venom. "Fuck you. Fuck you all."

Pete carefully wiped the spit from his face. His blue eyes turned a blazing red. "So be it." He sighed. "I gave you every chance. Every chance." Pete's placid face shifted into a mask of fury, and he roared at her. "EVERY CHANCE." His hand clasped around her throat, and he began to squeeze, choking the breath out of her. She could feel his fingers digging deep into her windpipe, crushing it like a blade of grass. She opened her mouth wide, gasping for air.

Pete smiled and parted his lips. A black cloud began to swirl and curl its way towards Beck's open mouth, sending out probing, gaseous tendrils. Beck struggled but Pete's vice-like grip didn't lessen. His mouth opened wider. In the cloud, Beck could see a twisting mass of images. Demons. Thousands of them. As they rushed towards her, she could hear their guttural voices filling the chamber.

"WE. ARE. LEGION."

"Oh no you don't, you motherfucker." The sharp crack of an M4 ricocheted through the chamber. "Get your filthy hands off her, you piece of shit." The bullet slammed through Pete's shoulder and into Beck's bullet-proof vest. For the umpteenth time in her life, Beck thanked the gods of Kevlar for keeping her breathing. The impact of Velasquez's bullet sent her and Pete spinning down to the ground.

The M4 barked repeatedly, double taps taking out all the remaining Lightbringers in quick succession. Velasquez was efficient, ruthless, and deadly accurate.

Pastor Reid, though, was a lot more difficult to hit. He dodged each bullet with an ease and oiled grace that belied the insane speed of his movements. He smiled lazily, grabbed Beck by her vest, and hurled her across the chamber as if she were a rag doll.

As Velasquez brought the M4 up again, Reid flicked a hand. The chamber seemed to shimmer and time slowed to a stop. Velasquez, frozen into position, could see, but couldn't move. Couldn't speak. Couldn't break her gaze from Reid.

Beck was locked in a split-second of time, suspended half-way up the wall where Reid had flung her. She too couldn't move a muscle, merely watch as Reid moved with a languid, fluid movement that reminded her of a cat idly playing with a soon-to-be-very-dead mouse.

On the ground, Pete looked up at his master. "My Lord."

Pastor Reid pressed a finger to his lips. "Shush, my child, shush." He bent down and smiled. His eyes blazed with a fiery red glow that bored into Pete's own orbs. "You've seen so much, haven't you, Pete? So much. You've seen the glories I offered you and your followers. You've seen the cleansing. You've been so fucking loyal to me, haven't you?" The smile started to melt away.

"You know that. I am always loyal to you."

Reid's smile vanished. "And yet, here we are. All your loyalty has left us with what, exactly? Nothing but interruptions and distractions." Reid stood back and glanced over at Beck. "I don't blame *you*. You're doing what any loving mother would do." He turned to Pete. "I blame you." He clamped a hand on Pete's face. The long, slim fingers twisted and bulged, the skin splitting like a ripe banana and allowing black, taloned claws to burst out. The hooked nails punctured Pete's skin, sending rivers of blood flowing down his face.

Pete tried to cry out but felt his jaw shatter in at least three places as Reid piled on the pressure. Reid picked up Pete by his face and held him inches from his own. A long, forked tongue uncoiled from between Reid's lips, and he slowly licked the blood from one of the puncture wounds. The tongue curled back into Reid's mouth, and he snarled. "This is all your fault."

Reid roared and crushed Pete's face like a grape. He hurled the twitching body into the pit, which sent up a rush of flames as if to welcome its newest victim. The chamber wall bulged and twisted. Pete's crushed, agony-filled face pressed against the black lava walls, letting out one last silent scream before vanishing back into the darkness.

Reid chuckled. "And now that's dealt with." He turned to Velasquez and smiled. "Did you really think bullets could do me any harm, child?"

"No. But I can."

Gabriel stepped into the chamber, flexed his fingers, and stood in front of Velasquez. He looked at Reid, taking in the demonic talon that wore the human skin of his host's hand like a tattered glove. He stared deep into the glowing red eyes filled with cruelty and violence.

And he smiled.

48

The wind sent a gust spiraling through the tops of the olive trees that surrounded Rancho Monteyo. A cloud of rooks leapt into the pre-dawn sky, circling the ranch house, and cawing loudly. In the stables, the horses snorted and whinnied, tramping their straw into the ground with flailing hooves.

Maria Monteyo sat bolt upright in bed, eyes wide open. She clutched the cross around her neck and gasped. "Gabriel." Her hand scrabbled on her nightstand, fingers searching desperately for her rosary. She felt the reassuring touch of the smooth beads on her skin and grasped the chain.

Feeding the rosary through her fingers, she began praying frantically.

49

Reid looked at Gabriel. "You have courage, monk, I'll give you that. Did your abbot teach you everything you needed to know, though, I wonder?" Reid chuckled.

Gabriel made the sign of the cross, which simply made Reid laugh louder. "Uh-oh, magic. Whatever shall I do? Mercy. Mercy." He roared with laughter. "Is that all you've got, monk? The sign of your dead master?"

"I think you called it a distraction." Gabriel stood with his hands on his hips. Behind him, Velasquez felt a tingle in her fingertips and could once again move. To her left she heard Beck slump to the ground and let out a sharp "Oof" as the air was knocked out of her lungs. "You see, as mighty as you may think you are, you're not yet strong enough to focus on more than one thing at a time." Gabriel scratched his nose. "A bit like a toddler, really. And that's all you are, isn't it? Right now, you're a mewling little toddler. So yes. It might be a simple thing, but it's enough." He glanced over to Velasquez. "Get her out of here. Now."

"Gabe."

"Go. Cathy's safe. Leave this demon to me." Gabriel fixed his gaze on Reid. "It won't take long."

Reid snarled. "I don't think they're going anywhere."

The chamber doorway was blocked with five children. A low, rolling growl filled the air, punctuated by hisses. The children opened their mouths, exposing rows of needle-sharp teeth. Their eyes glowed. Reid waved a hand towards Velasquez and Beck. "Feed, my children. Feed."

The children lunged at the two women.

50

Carver gunned the Range Rover along the track. There was no point in stopping to cover their tracks this time around. He reached the gate and hopped out of the driver's seat, leaving the engine running. It burbled quietly as he sprinted to the gate, found the carabiner that Velasquez had put in position, and undid it. He opened the gate and ran to the Range Rover.

As he clambered back into the driver's seat, he glanced towards the back seat.

It was empty.

"Shit." Carver looked around frantically. "Cathy? Hey, Cathy, sweetie, where are you? Not a good time to play peek-a-boo." He jumped out of the truck and looked around. "Cathy? C'mon, kid, I'm trying to help you." Carver heard the roof's metal skin bonging as a weight shifted. He looked up, straight into Cathy's face above him. Her eyes glowed and she let out a screech. The child leapt from the roof, her small fingers outstretched like tiny claws and landed on his shoulders. She slashed, bit, and clawed at Carver's face with the ferocity of a tiger cub.

"Jesus." Carver tried to hold her back, but she redoubled her attack with the force and power of a much larger creature. This was no kiddie's hissy fit. This was a demon attack that grew stronger and stronger every second.

For the first time in his life, Carver didn't know how to fight an opponent. What did he do? Did he grab the child and slap her unconscious? Did he try and restrain her? What the hell could he do?

51

T he orange glyphs on the chamber walls twisted and squirmed. Gabriel ignored the maelstrom that surrounded him and stepped forward. He pulled out a crucifix from his pocket and held it up. A bottle of holy water, conveniently housed in a squeegee bottle, appeared in his other hand. He sent a stream of holy water squirting towards Reid. It left a trail in the air like an arc of shimmering diamonds.

The water made contact with Reid. The demon inside him

roared and snarled, swiping at the droplets, and trying to wipe them away.

Gabriel squeezed the plastic bottle again and spoke in a loud voice. "In the name of the Father, and the Son, and the Holy Ghost, I bind you, unclean spirit and banish you back into the outer darkness."

"Is that any way to talk to an old friend?" Reid scratched idly at the patch of skin where the first jet of holy water had landed. The skin flaked and split, and he picked it off exposing the red muscle underneath.

"You're not my friend."

Reid adopted a tone like a buddy meeting a friend at a bar. "Sure we are. Have been for years. Don't you remember in high school when we first tried heroin together? Man, you got seriously into that shit, didn't you?" He laughed. "I mean, you loved that shit." He snarled. "How long did daddy have to keep you tied up in the barn 'til you got clean?"

Behind him, Gabriel could hear the children squealing as Velasquez mercilessly batted their attacks away. Beck shouted across as she untangled a furious little girl from around her neck and threw the child across the chamber. "He's trying to mess with you. Fight him. Jesus, will you get the FUCK off me, you little bitch."

Gabriel tried to block out the battle between his two friends and the children and focused on Reid. He knew what was happening. It was demoning 101. Get inside someone's head, mess with their confidence, make them doubt themselves.

He may have known exactly what Reid was doing, but that didn't make it any less painful to hear. He pushed down a boiling-hot wave of shame, trying to scour his father's face from his memory and refocus on banishing him before the entire mountainside went critical.

Reid saw the monk hesitate. He could almost hear Gabriel's internal monologue. The demon laughed and pushed harder. "And what about all those years in Iraq? How can a man of God reconcile the slaughter of innocents in the name of oil? Still can't get the stench of blood out of your nostrils, can you, soldier-boy?"

"Fight back." Velasquez slapped a pre-pubescent boy in the face hard enough to rock him back on his heels.

Reid went in for the kill. "And what about Al-Qa'im? Huh? Knowing your friend over there took a bullet meant for you? Does she know your dark shame? Does she know about the airstrike? About the school?" Reid glanced over to Beck. "Ever wonder why that village was so angry with you, Rebecca? Huh? Ever wonder why there were no children in that village? Why don't you ask him?" He pointed at Gabriel. "Why don't you ask him?"

Beck glared at Reid while holding a wriggling, hissing child at arm's length. "Because I know he's not a bullshitter, asshole. And you're just playing mind games, you little fuck."

Reid laughed. "Am I, though? And what about—"

Before Reid could finish, a roar of flames shot up from the center of the pit. Slowly, dripping globs of lava and molten skin, the lifeless body of Pete rose. Holding his disintegrating corpse was a giant, flame-colored talon. The talon encircled his entire torso, the long, hooked fingers splayed across the man's body. The hand squeezed and Pete's body crushed like an empty beer can. The hand tossed the remains across the chamber and gripped the edge of the pit. A second hand emerged from the pit. A massive, raven-like face with a vicious looking beak and huge horns appeared above the edge. The pit walls started to crumble and explode in a shower of shards that howled across the chamber like missiles. A huge torso followed the head, and on its back two massive wings unfurled. The demon kept on going up and up until it brushed the top of the chamber's bowed ceiling.

The demon looked around and picked up a lifeless Lightbringer. Opening its huge maw, it inserted the man's body headfirst, and bit down. It tossed the headless body to one side and spat the head out at Gabriel. The Lightbringer's head rolled to a stop at Gabriel's feet, the lifeless eyes staring up at the monk.

Reid smiled. "Now that's power."

Velasquez let out a yell and flicked the M4 to Rapid. She emptied every damn bullet she had into the creature. The bullets merely flattened and plopped harmlessly into the pit.

Reid held out a hand. "Gabriel? Meet Malphas. Malphas? My Lord? Meet Gabriel."

52

Cathy wouldn't quit. Her little nails might not have been the talons of Malphas, but they could still draw blood. Carver felt the stinging cat-scratches on his face and neck. He didn't want to hurt the child, she didn't know what she was doing. But this had to stop.

He reached back, grabbed her wrists, and bent forward, sending her screeching over the top of his head and down onto the ground. Shrieking, the child rolled like an expert and sprang onto all fours, hissing and snarling at Carver. She watched like a predator as Carver carefully moved towards the passenger door. He pushed it open and stood in front of the back seat. "C'mon, then."

Cathy let out a blood-curdling scream and sprang at Carver. At the last second, he moved out of the way and the child ended up on the back seat. Before she could leap out again, Carver slammed the door and hit the central locking button on his key fob. The alarm double-bleeped and the locks clicked into place. Cathy slammed her small body against the door, slapping her hands repeatedly on the window and squealing like a scalded cat. The big truck rocked and swayed as the child went berserk. Carver stepped away, unnerved by the repeated attempts of Cathy to break through the window. "Sorry. Really, I am. Just hold on in there, okay? Hold on in there, little one." Carver tried to make his voice as gentle as possible. The kid had been through hell. Literally. It wasn't her fault. As soon as Gabriel got back, they could get that son of a bitch demon out of her, and they'd have little Cathy back again.

Cathy. Beautiful little Cathy.

All blue eyes and curls. All smiles and kisses.

Carver looked at the incensed child and felt his heart break for her.

Cathy. Beautiful little possessed Cathy.

All glowing eyes and wild hair. All snarls and shrieks.

53

Gabriel stared at Malphas. Reid stood in front of his master, like a priest at the altar. He sneered at Gabriel. But Gabriel could see beyond that sneer. It was only there because Reid thought he'd won. Thought he'd brought Malphas into the world. Brought the fire. The burning. The start of Hell on Earth.

Yeah?

Well, here's the thing.

Gabriel had already seen Hell on Earth. It was a little village in Iraq called Al-Qa'im.

A piss-hole in the middle of the desert. Emaciated cattle and dead camels. Mud brick buildings and rusting pick-up trucks filled with "freedom fighters." An annex of Hell filled with dead bodies and clouds of flies.

Not caused by demons.

But by men.

This? Gabriel laughed out loud. This was amateur hour in comparison. Demons loved to show off. They went for the clichés. The brimstone and fire. The stink of sulfur. A bubbling pit? It was nothing. It was smoke and mirrors. It was nothing compared to what he'd seen simple, blue-collar men from Michigan and Idaho do when they were scared and only knew how to respond by unleashing the real demon inside. Not some clawed, needle-mawed monster. But the ability to kill a whole school full of children with a drone strike. A strike that should've hit a compound five miles away.

That? Yeah. That was Hell.

Not this carnival. This circus. Even Reid was joining in with the magic show, now, floating ten feet off the ground, arms outstretched like some sick parody of Christ risen. "Join us in the history books." Reid threw his head back and laughed.

Gabriel held up the crucifix, all the shame and humiliation melting away. In a moment of abject terror, facing down one of Hell's overlords, yards from the actual Pit of Hell, Gabriel Monteyo finally found peace. He felt it wash over him like a warm ocean wave. He could feel the power building inside him.

This was one strike that wasn't going to miss.

"You're already defeated, Malphas. You were when God cast

you all out of Heaven." His voice took on a deep, booming tone that echoed around the chamber.

Words have power.

Never underestimate them.

Never.

That's what the abbot had taught him. That's all the abbot needed to teach him. Find the right words and speak them with true passion. True feeling. True understanding. And say them with compassion.

Gabriel's voice rose. "And by His power I command you to leave here and return to Hell where you belong. By the power of Christ, I command you back into the Abyss. NOW."

The boom echoed around the chamber. It spilled out down the corridors and tunnels. As it reached each Lightbringer, it sent them crashing to their knees, holding their heads.

The shockwave hit those in the chamber hardest.

Reid threw back his head and screamed.

Malphas roared, the voice of the Legion bellowing through him.

The five children wailed in unison and fell to the ground.

Beck and Velasquez couldn't do anything except hold onto each other, huddled together, their heads bowed and fighting against the vortex of turmoil that tore at them.

And standing in a swirling, writhing mass of power stood Gabriel.

Serene.

Motionless.

Untouched by the raging storm that spiraled around him. He watched as Malphas snatched Reid from the air, let out a final bellow, and sank beneath the churning lava.

The children opened their mouths and five black clouds

poured out like angry bees, swarming, and swirling towards the pit before diving down into oblivion.

In a soft voice, he finished the incantation.

"Amen."

A swooping noise filled the chamber, followed by absolute silence. The only sound was the quiet sobbing of a little girl. Beck wrapped her arms around the child and held her close, soothing her and stroking her hair. "It's okay, little one."

She looked at Gabriel and smiled. "It's all over."

54

Cathy stopped her relentless beating on the window of the Range Rover. She sat back, eyes wide. Carver watched carefully, waiting to see if it was a trick.

Cathy opened her mouth and black smoke poured from between her lips. It filled the cabin and swirled around the child. Tendrils slammed against the glass again and again.

Carver hit the key fob and unlocked the doors. He grabbed

the handle and swore. It was red hot. Gritting his teeth, he pulled the door open and flung it as wide as he could.

The black cloud poured out of the cabin and shot up into the night sky, creating a vortex above the old mine.

It couldn't find a way in.

It was trapped in a world where it didn't belong. A denizen of Hell alone in the world of men. A scream echoed through the dawn air and the cloud zoomed away over the horizon. Carver watched it go. "Shit. Shit." He ran his hand through his hair. "Guess that's unfinished business, then."

"I want my mommy."

Carver snapped his attention away from the demon cloud to Cathy. The little girl looked at him through bright blue eyes. Gone were the harrowing red dots of the demon. Now she was herself again. Beautiful little Cathy. And she wanted her mommy.

Carver scooped her up into his arms and hugged her tight. "So do I, sweetie. He kissed her forehead and smiled at her. "Shall we go find mommy together, huh? Waddya say?"

Cathy smiled and nodded, sniffling the last of her tears away. She flung her arms around Carver's neck and burrowed her head into his shoulder.

Carver carried her around to the passenger side and sat her down, carefully buckling the seatbelt. He smiled again and ruffled her curls. "Ready?" Cathy nodded happily. "Okay, then." He trotted around to the driver's door, hopped in, and started the engine. He threw Cathy a reassuring smile. "Let's go."

The Range Rover wheel-spun away from the track and onto the road towards the rendezvous point.

55

The chamber looked smaller.

Without the demon, the boiling pit, and the floating pastor, it looked empty. The orange glyphs had faded into the blackness. The once solid blocks of stone that lined the pit were cracked and broken. The huge tiles that spiraled around the floor in a concentric pattern now looked dirty and uneven.

Gabriel stood in the middle of the chamber and breathed

deeply. There was still a faint tang of sulfur in the air. That cordite smell you got after an explosion.

Explosion.

NO.

Gabriel snapped out of his requiem of calm back to the here and now. He may have just banished one of Hell's A-listers back to the inferno, but unless they made tracks fast, they'd be joining Malphas. He spun around. "Get the kids and anyone you see along the way. We've got to get out of here right now."

Velasquez looked at him. "Why?"

"Because the entire place is wired to blow, that's why." He glanced around the chamber. Sure enough, sitting unobtrusively in a corner sat a white plastic box. He ran over to it and flipped open the lid. A digital timer winked in the half-light.

09:59.

"We have less than ten minutes."

Beck herded the children together. The little girl started crying again. Beck crouched and smoothed her hair away from her face. "I bet you're really good at running, aren't you?" She gave the little girl a smile. The child nodded through her tears. "Wanna show me?" Beck stood and held out her hand. The little girl slipped her own tiny hand into Beck's and held on tight.

Velasquez glanced at Gabriel and nodded. "Okay, kids. Ready? Set, GO."

They ran out of the chamber and along the tunnel. The lights were starting to flicker.

Topside, the Lightbringers were trying to come to terms with not having superhuman powers anymore, or indeed, any sense of purpose. They were confused, frightened, and useless.

Their lack of focus included losing the ability to keep the generator running.

In the mine, Beck, Velasquez, Gabriel, and the children reached the shaft. "Up. Then left. And keep going. The exit isn't far. Velasquez, you go first. Keep the kids together."

Velasquez nodded and scrambled up the ladder. She flopped down onto her belly at the top and beckoned. The oldest children started climbing. "One at a time. The ladder's pretty strong, but you need to go one at a time." She tried to make her voice as reassuring as she could. They weren't dealing with demons anymore. Just frightened kids.

Gabriel was the last to climb the ladder. It creaked and groaned under his weight. The rust-riddled rungs hadn't seen this much action since the old timers left the place decades before. The crumbling bolts holding the ladder to the wall started to pull away. He was almost at the top.

"Come on." Beck held out a hand, frantically motioning at him to climb.

Gabriel could have sworn that he felt a taloned hand grab at his clothes, trying to pull him back down into the abyss.

He yelped as a key bolt sheared clean away. The ladder started to fall back. He threw his hand up and felt Beck catch his wrist. The rotten ladder tumbled into the flickering darkness and Gabe hung in mid-air. Beck let out a yell. "I can't hold him."

Velasquez clamped her hands on Gabriel's arm and the two women hauled Gabriel up the last few feet. He felt as if his arm was being pulled out of its socket. The women were running on pure adrenaline. But he had to make the lip of the shaft before it gave out and they lost their grip on him. He swung his other arm up and felt Velasquez shift her grip. With a firm hold on both his wrists, the two women hauled him over the edge of the shaft and onto the ground. He scrambled away from the shaft and lay on his back for a moment, breathing heavily. Gabriel turned his head towards Beck. "I never did like heights."

"It's not heights that kill you. It's the sudden stop at the bottom." Beck stood and held out a hand. "Tick-tock."

Gabriel clamped his hand into Beck's, and she hauled him to his feet. Gabriel looked at the group. "Not far now."

In the chamber, the digital counter hit 02:59.

56

Carver watched as dawn started to break over the
mine. Through his binoculars, he could see people
pouring into the compound, blinking in the light.
The air was filled with the sound of sirens as police cars, fire
trucks and ambulances screeched up the road towards the
compound.

Carver shifted his gaze to the side exit from the mine, well
away from the main compound. His hands tensed around the

binoculars. "Where are you?" He scanned the area again. The emergency vehicles were pouring through the gate and screeching to a halt in the compound. He could see first responders dashing among the ex-Lightbringers, shepherding them to safe areas away from the main pit entrance.

Carver refocused his attention to the side exit. A grin split his face. "YES. YES." He tossed the binoculars into the Range Rover and jumped in. He turned to Cathy and gave her a huge smile. "Mommy's coming, sweetie. Mommy's coming."

He gunned the engine and slid onto the blacktop, fishtailing the big truck, and leaving stripes of rubber on the surface.

57

G abriel lifted the last of the kids out of the exit and into the early morning sunlight. He gave the mine one last glance and made the sign of the cross.

Not everyone would get out.

May God have mercy on their souls.

58

I n the chamber, the digital counter hit 00:00.
The world stopped.
And then exploded.

59

Explosions shook the compound like a series of earthquakes. Emergency personnel and Lightbringers were flung to the ground. Those closest to the east shaft ran for their lives as a mushroom of flames billowed out of the shaft entrance and into the air. A series of explosions sent pits of the compound collapsing into the underground voids. The west shaft belched its own mushroom-shaped fire cloud, igniting the scrub around the compound.

Mayhem and chaos took hold. The fire crews desperately started fighting the eruptions of flames that shot into the air. Because the blasts couldn't go outwards, they went up and sideways, finding any exit point they could. Columns of superheated air and fire shot into the air.

At the east exit, Gabriel yelled at everyone to get away from the entrance. They dived for cover as a bloom of fire burst through the exit. The flames retreated into the mine and the rumble of a total collapse sent out a cloud of choking dust. "Make for the road." Gabriel waved his arm. "Make for the road."

At that second, Carver screeched to a halt. He wound down the window and grinned. "Need a ride?"

Velasquez and Gabriel herded the children into the back seat and shut the door. Gabriel climbed in and sat with two little girls and a young boy on his lap. Two older children snuggled up to him, too shell-shocked to speak.

Velasquez walked around to the driver's door and laid a hand on Carver's cheek. "Nice timing, butch."

"Any time, sugar."

Beck stumbled through the scrub towards the truck. She wrenched open the passenger door, yelling. "Cathy. CATHY."

"Mommy."

Cathy. Beautiful little Cathy.

All blue eyes and curls. All smiles and kisses.

Beck burst into tears and swept Cathy up in her arms. She sobbed, clinging to the little girl. "Mommy's here, baby. Mommy's here." She kissed her again and again. "And I'm never letting you go again, baby, you hear me? Never." She felt the little girl wrap her arms around her neck and hold on tight. Cathy buried her head in her mother's shoulder and whispered.

"I love you, mommy."

60

The vineyard was empty of visitors. Gray clouds lined the California sky and a gentle rain fell. The vines had been harvested for the year. Only a few birds hopped among the trellises, feeding on discarded grapes and the occasional bug. The birds looked up as the sound of a Jeep punching through the gears drifted across the valley.

On the road, Beck drove the Jeep up the hill towards the

monastery, the slap-slap of her windshield wipers in almost perfect time with the beat of her heart.

Slow.

Steady.

The beat of a heart that's at peace.

Beck turned in and drove past the visitor parking area. She stopped in an empty gravel lot, the tires crunching on the stones and sending them scattering. She killed the engine and hopped out, making a dash for the dry sanctuary of the visitor center.

She opened the door, turned, and shook herself like a dog, sending droplets of water spraying across the glass door panel. The monk behind the cash register smiled. "I take it he's expecting you this time?"

"Hello, Friar Tuck. Still here then, I see?" Beck smiled at the young monk.

"It's Brother Marcus, Miss Beck." The monk gave her a gentle grin back. "I'll go get him for you."

"No need. I know the way."

The monk smiled again. "Of course you do. Go with God."

Beck nodded. "And you, kiddo." She strolled through the "STAFF ONLY" door and walked quickly along the corridor to the cloister garden. She stopped at the entrance.

There he was.

Sitting there, in his habit, staring at the rain from the shelter of an overhang.

He looked at peace.

Wordlessly, Beck walked over and sat next to Gabriel. For a moment, neither spoke.

"How's Cathy?" Gabriel stared into the garden, watching a bird splashing about happily in the bird bath.

"Fine. I don't think she remembers much." Beck stared at the bird too, watching the droplets of water arc in the air like diamonds.

"And that's why you didn't bring her."

"No point in poking the bear. She'll have to pay enough in therapy when she's older."

Gabriel smiled. "She can always come here. Sometimes a safe place and some peace are all you need."

"Is that all you need?"

Gabriel turned to her. "It's all I've ever wanted. After everything we've been through, don't you think we deserve a little peace?"

"I guess."

The two friends were silent for a few minutes before Gabriel spoke again. "The other kids?"

"Their parents were among the survivors. Luckily."

"So you believe in luck now?"

Beck sighed. "No. I used to. I don't know what I believe in anymore."

Gabriel reached out and took her hand. "Believe in yourself. Believe in Cathy. Believe in right." He sighed. "We've all got demons we're afraid of. You and me perhaps more than most. But what we did was for the good of everyone."

"So all of that bullshit was God's will then, monk?"

"No." Gabriel laughed. "But I'm sure He had a hand in it somewhere." He gave Beck's hand a squeeze. "All that bullshit, as you call it, was willed by men. Stupid men who wanted power. Power they couldn't possibly hope to control. This wasn't about demons and gods, Rebecca. It was about people."

Beck nodded. She sighed. "Velasquez and Carver say hi."

Gabriel smiled broadly. "Say hi to them for me."

"Velasquez says there's a chair for you at the weekly poker game if you want."

"Old snake-eyes Velasquez?" Gabriel laughed. "No thanks. This gig includes a vow of poverty, I'm afraid."

"With Velasquez playing, that wouldn't be a problem." Beck grinned. "I could spot you."

"No thanks. I'd rather not be in your debt again."

Beck turned to Gabriel, her face serious. "You aren't. You never were. You never will be in my debt. You get that? You need anything, anything, you call me. You call us. We'll be there. No questions. Like it's always been. No debts between friends."

Silence descended. The pitter-patter of the rain drummed softly on the leaves. In the birdbath, the bird let out a chirrup of song, the notes trilling through the cloister and into the California air.

A bell sounded, melodic and deep. Gabriel stood. "Afternoon prayers. Join me?"

"No thanks. But remember me in your prayers, yeah?"

"Always." He wrapped his arms around Beck and held her close. Gently, he kissed her forehead. "Go with God."

She looked up at him and smiled, her eyes lined with tears. "You, too." She grinned mischievously and abruptly turned to walk through the cloister and out the visitor center.

Gabriel climbed the stairs and watched her drive away. The abbot joined him. "A troubled soul, Brother Gabriel."

Gabriel smiled as the Jeep disappeared into the distance. "Once, maybe." He turned and looked at the abbot. "But not anymore." He motioned to the doorway. "Shall we?"

The rain stopped, and the clouds broke, allowing a ray of sunshine to shine down like a bolt of lightning.

A thousand miles away, a black, swirling cloud found a cave in Italy and burrowed deep into the darkness to wait.

THE END